HEART
TO
HEART

by

Marcella DiPaolo

ISBN-13: 978-1-64395-012-9 (Kindle eBook)
ISBN-13: 978-1-64395-112-6 (Paperback)

For copyright permission requests, or for information about special discounts available for bulk purchases, sales promotions, or educational needs, write to or e-mail the publisher at one of the following addresses.

Phantasy Publishing LLC
35 Brooks Drive
Bethalto, IL 62010

Website: www.phantasypublishing.com
E-mail: support@phantasypublishing.com

This is a work of fiction. Names, characters, places, and incidents are either the products of the author's imagination, or they are used fictitiously. Any resemblance to actual persons, living or dead, businesses, companies, events, or locales is entirely coincidental.

Published in the United States of America

Table of Contents

CHAPTER 1

Hazel eyes stared back at the young girl as she took one last look at her reflection. Gazing critically at the wisps of soft brown hair framing her face, Beth sighed. "It won't be long now," she murmured. Picking up her purse, she moved to the door of her tiny basement apartment. Closing the door carefully behind her, listening for the click which told her it was locked, listening for what may be the last time she would hear the lock on her home, she quietly walked up the stairs and towards the front door.

She paused at her landlord's door, wondering if she should make one last attempt to gain time. Surely, she'd be able to find work somewhere, doing something useful. Her savings were running out and next month's rent would be due on Friday. Taking a deep breath, Beth decided to tackle her landlord after seeing Uncle Henry, who knows, maybe he really did have a solution. She walked out into the bright March morning.

The street was already alive with people hurrying to work amidst the tree lined streets. Small stores dotted the sidewalks of the closely spaced buildings, the brick sidewalks remnants of past times. Once a prospering suburb, the houses still had a cared for look. Many of the older, larger homes were much too expensive to be inhabited by only one family and duplexes and rentals were common sites up and down the block.

Beth walked quickly now, hearing the bus nearing her corner. Seeing her approach, the kindly driver waited while Beth ran the last steps and climbed the stairs, smiling her thanks to the driver, the doors closed behind her. Finding a seat during rush hour was not that easy and finally Beth clutched the strap and resolved to stand for her short trip. "Two more stops," Beth thought. Her forehead creased with worry. Too wrapped up in her own thoughts, Beth did not notice the appreciative glances of several men as they watched her slim body sway as the bus lumbered along. Beth was unaware of the appealing waif-like look of her hazel eyes and wispy hair curling attractively about her face, or of the inborn grace which accompanied her every movement.

The bus was moving into a very prosperous part of town, a shopping center marking the hub of many drives and rides. "One more stop," thought Beth. Today is the day I have to have a solution to my problem. Uncle Henry's call last night sounded so strange. He's such a darling but how can he possibly help? Oh well, it certainly can't hurt to go see him before I come to any conclusions or decisions.

Beth walked to the front of the bus and walked down the stairs. Turning to the right she saw, high above the heads of the passersby, a newly painted billboard. Pain etched across Beth's face. That could be me she thought. Shaking her head again, no, it can't or won't ever again. Too many scars were there to make it me, she thought. How cruel fate could be! Only a few months ago that was my name and my picture on that same billboard. My opening night, an opening night doomed before it even began. All too clearly that night flashed before her eyes as it had so many times since, becoming a living nightmare for many months.

Her opening night as a singer in a small, exclusive, downtown nightclub, with Johnny playing accompaniment on the piano. A childhood dream, she was finally a star, or soon would be the reviews said, Elizabeth Riley, a very gifted and aspiring young singer the papers had written. As lovely to behold as she was to listen to. Beth could still hear the applause that night, as song after song she grew more confident. Dressed in a pale golden gown, she had glittered and captured the hearts of all as she sang ballads, country, modern medleys and her own songs. She was on her last song when smoke was first noticed. Stay calm, Beth remembered saying and continued singing to maintain that calm.

Everyone was almost out. Beth was rushing off the stage with Johnny when the smoke became too much. Crawling on all fours, she had half dragged, half carried him to the door. The roof came down minutes later catching Beth even as she was dragged from the building by the firemen. Burns covered parts of her body and smoke had damaged her lungs. But with the scars she would carry forever was the fear that never again would she ever go on a stage again. The papers called her courageous, but she knew what a coward she really was.

For weeks she was cared for in the burn center of the hospital. Then came the months of skin grafts and therapy. On the outside she looked the same, but Beth was very much aware of the scars on her shoulders and on her back. Scars which will probably always be there the doctor said. But with time they will fade. Maybe,

Beth often thought, but the scars in my mind will never go away.

"Never will I go on a stage and sing. I've tried, God help me, I've tried." she cried. Still feeling the panic rising deep within her, she stood before the faceless audience. Cold sweat breaking across her face and body, nausea rising from the pain, and running from the stage or rather led by Johnny. I was even too petrified to move, Beth thought bitterly. Courageous? Hardly, I can't even sing for my supper!

Her pale green suit, the fitted jacket, the ruffled print and green blouse emphasized her shapely body, as slender legs peeped beneath the swirling pleated skirt. The crisp air caused a flush to the pale cheeks. The heart-shaped face with the large hazel eyes and delicate lips was surrounded by creamy white skin. A slight smattering of freckles covered the small pert nose and her light brown hair was feathered back from her face, the heavy thick mane falling in a disarray of soft curls to her shoulders.

Beth walked resolutely to the elevator, pushed the fourth-floor button and waited for the elevator to close. As the doors began to move, she heard a voice, "hold the door, please." A young lady arrived out of breath holding the hand of a toddler. "I just can't seem to get anywhere on time," she sighed. "Especially when I'm carrying the extra baggage of these two."

Beth smiled, first at the flustered mother and next at the little girls. "Which floor?" questioning eyes were raised to the young girls. "Fourth," she answered. "We're buying a house, contract for deed. My husband is to meet us here at 9:30. Our sitter called at the last minute and cancelled so, I've brought our two monkeys with us. I'm not sure how much we'll get done, but I just couldn't call and cancel. It means too much to us to get it all done and at least get the paperwork out of the way."

As the elevator doors opened, both girls started walking toward the same corridor and as luck would have it, the same door. On impulse Beth turned toward the girl and said, "We seem to have the same destination. My appointment is for 9:00. Why don't you take my time, I'll watch your little ones and then I'll go in later?

"No, I couldn't impose on you that way, I hardly know you!"

"If it makes it any easier, Henry Daniels is my uncle. He'll vouch for me and besides which I would love the few extra minutes to marshal my thoughts before I see him today. I really wouldn't volunteer you know unless I wanted to! "

"Well," the young mother began only to stop and smile at the young man waiting outside the door. Obviously, her husband, as he hurried forward and took the toddler by the hand.

"The sitter cancelled, Richard," at his answering frown, "I thought it best to come rather than cancel. Mr. Daniel's niece was just offering to watch them for us while we get the paperwork done."

"Thank you," he said smiling, "We can finish so much faster without the little ones climbing about. We'll hurry, promise." Smiling their thanks, the young parents preceded Beth into the office. Beth smiled at Uncle Henry's secretary, "We're switching appointments, Grace, if that's OK. It'll give me more time with Uncle Henry."

Grace smiled, "That will be fine, Elizabeth! Sit down please, Mr. Daniels will see you in a moment."

Seating themselves in the comfortable waiting room, the children looked carefully around. Their names were Emily and Sara their mother was saying. Beth nodded and smiled. Picking up a book she asked Emily if she would like her to read a story to her.

Dimples formed on either side of her tiny mouth as she nodded "yes" and joyfully climbed up on Beth's lap. The baby Sara was asleep, and the young couple decided to take her with them as their names were called into Uncle Henry's office. Beth smiled at Emily and began to read, "Once upon a time in the forest lived three bears ... " Halfway through the story another person entered. Hearing the door open Beth looked up. Her eyes met the cold, hard stare of dark blue eyes. Eyes that held her as if hypnotized.

Emily looked too, the stare of a child. "Oh, look at his face!" she cried. Beth's eyes left his and saw his face as well. A large jagged scar went from his cheek down to his neck. Beth leaned to the little girl and said, "We all have scars, love, some are just more easily seen than others. But scars don't make people, it's what's under them that you have to see." Beth looked up to see those eyes staring at her. She hadn't intended him hearing her explanation. A flush crept under her skin as he continued to stare. The blue eyes missed nothing in their appraisal of the young girl holding the toddler. Beth was unaware of the attractive picture they made. Unaware of the thoughts running quickly through the stranger's mind, with quick easy strides he walked to the secretary, spoke to her and sat down.

As he had turned, Beth took the opportunity to look at the man. He's very big, Beth thought, at least 6'3" or 6'4". His muscular body showing beneath the suit he wore. His skin tanned to a bronze color and his hair so dark as to look almost blue in the lights. He turned, catching her stare. Embarrassed, Beth proceeded to read to Emily. She had just finished when Uncle Henry's door opened, and Emily's parents hurried out. "Thank you ever so much," she said. "Have you been a good girl, Em?"

"She's been a doll," Beth grinned. "I wouldn't mind keeping her."

The young husband grinned in response. "You'd soon send her back. Let's go, crew, I've got time for a treat with you before I'm due back at work!"

As they walked out, Uncle Henry came to the door. "Beth, come on in." He smiled from ear to ear, but his smile faded somewhat as he saw the stranger. Beth noticed the stranger give a slight nod to her uncle. Uncle Henry nodded in return. On the surface, it looked like a mere common courtesy of acknowledgement, but something wasn't quite right. Beth felt uneasy going into Henry's office. Shaking aside her confused thoughts, she kissed her uncle's cheek and sat down. "Hi love, now what's so important that you called and rushed me over here this morning?"

Uncle Henry smiled, swallowed hard, "Have you come up with a job?" At her shake of her head, he continued, "Before I begin Beth, I want you to promise to hear me out...the whole story--until I've finished telling you everything. It's important and I really feel the solution to your circumstances. Will you promise, Beth?"

7

Beth's strange uneasiness grew, "I promise to listen, Uncle Henry," she said slowly.

"Good." Taking a deep breath Uncle Henry began. "Since your accident you've had some trouble getting a job. Being prepared to be a singer, you never had any training to do anything else. Now that your singing career is over, it's made it difficult in finding anything you can do well. I know of your many talents Beth, you cook, sew, paint, you can charm young and old alike, but those aren't the kind of talents that people hire others for. In the terms of your parents' will, you can't have the money your parents left you until you're 25, that's three more years. We both know your savings won't hold you over until then. We've told you you're welcome with us, but I know that fierce Riley pride won't let you. I've been looking over the will, there is one clause that we've overlooked in the past that would change things."

"Uncle Henry, we went over the will with a fine-tooth comb, it's unbreakable, you said so yourself," Beth murmured.

"Unbreakable yes, but not unalterable. The will does state that if you were to marry and stay married for a year all the money would go immediately to you."

"Uncle Henry, I'm not in love with anyone nor can I imagine anyone in the future who would take a scarred misfit for a wife. I'm sorry, love, I just don't see this as a solution to my problem." She started to rise, but his arm detained her.

"Beth, you promised to wait until I was finished, remember?" He paused. As he did, Beth sat back down. Starting again, he said, "I know you want to marry for love, we all do, but what if I could arrange a marriage of convenience to last only for a year, no strings attached?

I have a client who needs a wife, in name only so to speak, to help him out of a legal matter as well. You both need a year to satisfy the courts of your marriage. He's a good man, Beth, or I wouldn't even be suggesting this. At the end of one year you both will have attained what you need, and you can part, no strings attached."

"Uncle Henry do you honestly expect me to marry a man I've never met simply to get my hand on the money!   And if I did agree to this preposterous idea, what exactly happens during that year? We part after our nuptials and say 'Adios, see you around!' Also, why can't this fellow find himself a wife? Is he so hard up he has to buy a wife this way?" Beth stopped to catch her breath, her mind whirling. This was ludicrous. How could Uncle Henry even suggest such a thing? How could anyone marry someone they've never met?!

"Beth, hear me out, please. I know it's out of the ordinary but there are reasons. It won't hurt to listen will it?" He looked at Beth and saw her shake of the head. Sitting down, he took off his glasses and rubbed his eyes. "Let me continue. This client has a brother, or rather had one. About a month ago his brother and his wife were killed, a plane crash. They left behind two small children. The will places the children in my client's hands only if he's married. Otherwise they go to the wife's sister. Before you can say anything, let me tell you about the sister. She is a beautiful, wealthy woman. She is also selfish, greedy and totally without any feeling for the needs of the two small children. The only reason the sister wants the children is because she has a need for revenge on my client. He was once pursued by many beautiful women, she was one of them, he gave

9

her the cold shoulder so to speak and has never been forgiven or forgotten."

"If he was pursued by so many beautiful women, why not choose one of those, why a stranger?"

"Several years ago, my client was a successful football star. He had an accident. One which left him scarred and out of a profession. His fiancé dumped him. He became a recluse. It was only when his brother died that he came out of his hermitage so to speak. He hasn't been in touch with any of those women since and has no desire to. He wants to come out of this year marriage without any strings too. He doesn't have a very high opinion of women, this sister-in-law, his fiancé, and even his own mother left him and his brother to fend for themselves at an early age. His will stipulates he must be married and living in the old homestead of his grandparents for one year, at that time the children are legally his. No court hassles, but if at any time his sister-in-law can prove that he's not, he loses all claim. The farm is one they grew up on in a place in Illinois, off the Mississippi River. A little place called Elsah. It hasn't been lived in for several years and needs a lot of work. You would be expected to live there and only spend the money earned from the farm. It's a strange will, but one which will definitely get his brother out of his hermit's existence and also provide a very favorable setting for the two young children. They're very confused right now. Jennifer is only four and Michael is five. You remember how you felt when your own parents were killed, and you weren't much older. They need someone who really cares about them. That's why I thought of you. Before you make up your mind, let me introduce you to my client."

10

He rose and went to the door. Beth's thoughts were on the children. How can I possibly do this she thought, and how can I not do it? She looked up as Uncle Henry's client came to the door. "Beth, I'd like you to meet Murphy Whitaker."

Cold blue eyes stared at Beth. "Well," the stranger said, "is it to be yes or no?" No preliminaries, no greeting, just the question.

Beth thought of those two little children alone with the sister or alone with this cold stranger. She shivered as she rose, looking him squarely in the eyes and without smiling, Beth replied, "It is to be yes."

CHAPTER 2

"You will be landing at St. Louis Lambert Airport in two hours. Lunch will be served in fifteen minutes. If you need anything, let us know. Thank you for flying ..."

As the voice of the captain droned on, Beth glanced at the stranger beside her, no stranger anymore, her husband of about one hour. "Oh God, what have I done?" she thought. Her mind retraced the last few days beginning with her decision to say yes to the entire proposition.

"Is it to be yes out of pity, or out of greed, Miss Riley?"

"Neither," Beth replied. "Unless it's the pity I feel for two young children thrown at the mercy of a cold heartless bachelor or his mercenary sister-in-law. Children need warmth and love Mr. Whitaker, and I don't think you're capable of giving either!" Flushed from her outburst, she glared back at Murphy willing him to speak.

"Your motives are admirable, Miss Riley, but much too good to be true. I see no wings; therefore, you can't be an angel, no halo, you can't be a saint, I trust that therefore makes you human like the rest of us. Your holier than thou attitude is not going to make for marital bliss but seeing as you're only a woman, what could I expect." Turning to Uncle Henry, Murphy Whitaker offered his hand, "Thank you, Daniels, I think.

It takes three days for blood tests; we'll be married by the Justice of the Peace on Friday morning at 10:00. Following our marriage, we'll board the airplane for St. Louis. I believe there is a plane leaving at noon. We should arrive about 2:30 at the Lambert Airport. I'll have a car waiting and we'll immediately drive to Elsah. It's about a three-hour drive from St. Louis, so we should arrive at the homestead by 6:00 at least. I trust you can make whatever arrangements need to be done to leave in three days' time?"

This time the question was leveled at her. Beth squared her shoulders, clicked her heels together and offered a military salute to Murphy, "Aye, aye, captain," she quipped.

Cold blue eyes again fastened themselves on Beth, silence followed her remark. Turning his head to Uncle Henry, he nodded and walked from the room.

Uncle Henry turned to Beth, a slow impish grin began to turn up his mouth at the corners, "Oh girl, when I first thought of this situation, I had grave misgivings that Murphy would put a damper on that lovely Irish wit, but now I fear it's Murphy I should have the misgivings for. And far from the calm, quiet year he expected, I'm sure you'll give just as good as you get!" Uncle Henry gathered Beth to him, and both laughed. But she remembered those eyes staring at her and an ice-cold tremor flowed up her spine. "Well," Beth thought, "I may not win, but I'll definitely give Murphy Whitaker a run for his money."

During the next three days thoughts of those dark blue eyes haunted Beth. She packed her few belongings, notified her landlord, and went shopping for her wedding dress at Uncle Henry's insistence. "It ought to be black," Beth thought, "or at least dark blue to match his eyes. Perhaps a dress of solid ice to match his wide unwavering stare." Walking up and down the streets, Beth became exhausted from looking for a dress she really didn't feel like buying. "Oh, bother the man, he won't care or notice anyway. I could wear a gunny sack!" Beth was even angrier because for a reason she couldn't fathom that thought bothered her. Turning the corner, Beth noticed a small boutique on the corner of the mall. Might as well since I'm here and walked into the front.

She was met by a saleswoman immediately. "May I help you?"

"Yes," Beth answered, "I'm looking for a dress to wear to a wedding. I want something special and yet I want to be able to wear it again."

"Did you have a specific color or style in mind?"

"A cream or off-white, maybe a wispy layered dress or a suit? I really don't know, but I'll know it when I see it." Beth smiled, "I'm not much help, am I?"

The saleswoman studied Beth a moment, one hand on her hip, the other held her chin. "Just a moment." She disappeared to the back of the store. Moments later she returned carrying a dress covered with plastic. "This came by mistake. We don't usually sell these, but if it suits, we won't have to send it back." As she took off the plastic, Beth gasped. The dress was beautiful. It was a cream-colored chiffon. Long full sleeves shimmered with an unseen silver thread. The round collar was edged with a tiny row of lace. The skirt was layers of chiffon, gently gathered.

"I love it," Beth murmured, "if it fits, this is it." Slipping it on in the fitting rooms, it seemed as if the dress were made for her. It emphasized the graceful curves of her body, the slender legs. "I'll take it," Beth told the saleswoman. "It's perfect."

Again, the saleslady studied Beth, "Is this to be your wedding?"

"Yes," Beth smiled, "it is."

"Wait just one more minute, if you would." Again, she disappeared into the back room. When she emerged, she was carrying a box? "These also came with the dress." She opened the box. Lying inside was a ringlet of silk flowers, pale lilacs, lilies of the valley, violets, it was a creation of simple flowers. Beside it lay a small matching bouquet of flowers. Beth's eyes glowed. Looking at the flowers she thought of the surprise she would find in those cold dark blue eyes when he saw her at 10:00 tomorrow morning.

"Wrap them up," she told the clerk, "You've just completed my ensemble!"

Uncle Henry was there promptly at 9:30 on Friday morning. When he saw Beth, he stopped. His eyes misted over, and he swallowed hard. "My God child, you are the most beautiful bride a groom could envision. Your parents would be so proud of you at this moment. You've done us all very proud, lass. Before we go," he wiped his eyes with his handkerchief, "if you ever need anything, need to get away, don't you hesitate to call me. If it weren't for that damn Irish pride, you'd have let me help you all along! I love you child, you know that, just see that you don't forget it."

Beth leaned forward and gently kissed his cheek. "And I love you Uncle Henry, and all you've done for me since my parents died. Don't you forget about me just because I'm an old married lady, okay? We'd better go now, unless we're to keep 'his majesty' waiting. How would that look, late for my own wedding!?" Beth laughed, a nervous sound, "I don't think Murphy would wait for us!"

Uncle Henry joined in her laughter and they walked out the door. "No, I don't think he would. Don't fear girl, like I told you, Murphy is a good man, he's grown bitter and cynical over the years since his accident, but underneath he's one of the best there is. How many men would give up their bachelor days to care for two children he's never met? He loved his brother and he'll make sure that no harm comes to them for his brother's memory if for no other reason. He'll also take care of you lass, he's a man of his word."

They traveled to the courthouse in silence. Arriving with only a few minutes to spare, Beth noticed Murphy standing on the steps, watching, hands in his pockets causing the suit to strain under his muscular shoulders. For a time both Beth and Murphy stared at each other, he at the vision of loveliness. A ray of sunshine seemed to circle her hair causing it to shine, the wreath of flowers circling her head giving her an ethereal appearance. Her eyes were soft and shining, her face upturned to catch his gaze. Her body was slim, and her curves were delicately outlined beneath the soft folds of chiffon. Murphy caught his breath and took a step forward to meet them. He stopped himself just in time. Beautiful she may look, but he knew about beauty, and he was not to be fooled again.

Beth had watched Murphy, seen his eyes look on her, saw a light appear in their cold dark depths. A flood of happiness flowed through her, and just as quickly she saw him take that step forward and return to the cold hard look she remembered so well. Murphy shook hands with Uncle Henry and again looked at Beth. The light appeared again in his eyes, making them warm and soft.

"My God," Beth thought, "I could drown in those depths." She smiled, a slow smile starting in her eyes and ending in the dimple showing in her left cheek. For one second Murphy returned that smile, changing his hard features into a softer image. For the first time Beth noticed the grey covering his temples, the even white teeth and the barest hint of a curl in that raven dark hair.

Murphy's smile faded as he offered Beth his arm. "No last-minute change of mind," he said.

"No, disappointed?" Beth answered and together they entered the courthouse. Minutes later her voice had trembled slightly as she pronounced her vows of love, honor and obedience to a total stranger, a stranger whose eyes were beginning to haunt her.

Beth shook her head, to clear it of the memory of those soft, warm blue eyes she had glimpsed. Turning to her companion on the plane she spoke softly, "Murphy, would you like to tell me now just what you want of me. Shouldn't I know about the farm in Elsah, and the children, and the plans you've made, and it also probably wouldn't hurt if you mentioned your sister-in-law just so that I can be prepared."

Her hazel eyes looked up into the face of her husband. Murphy made no comment. Taking a deep breath Beth continued, "Okay, no help from you. Let's adlib my first meeting with your sister in law! 'Why hello, can't say I'm glad to meet you, I've heard you're such a bitch. May I call you sis? I don't know your name. I'm confident we can be good enemies if we both just try.'" Beth raised a laughing face to her husband. "Will that do, dear?"

"Perfectly," Murphy replied, a slow smile breaking his autocratic face. "I've known her for years, and that's about as good an introduction as anyone could do, without being hypocritical, of course. You've made your point. We're almost ready to land. As soon as we're in the car, I'll talk. Okay, Bride?"

"Okay, husband," Beth gripped. She picked up her book and started to read. She stole a quick glance at Murphy, surprising his slow appraisal of her. Blushing, she whispered, "Do I pass inspection, sir?"

For the first time Murphy chuckled. "I think you'll do; we just might pull this off after all."

His faint praise had Beth suddenly feeling very good. At the back of her mind a tiny voice seemed to ask why should she care so much about what he thought of her? Minutes later, the pilot's voice came over the intercom, "We shall be landing in St. Louis in five minutes, please fasten your seat belts. Please refrain from smoking until further notice. Thank you for flying with us." Following a smooth landing, Murphy and Beth tracked down their luggage. "Where to now?" Beth asked. "Do we rent a car, call a cab or walk?"

Murphy answered, "None of the above. Follow me." Without a backward glance Murphy strode off. His long, powerful steps hard enough for Beth to keep up with by herself, but carrying her cases, she soon began to fall behind. All of the people in the airport suddenly seemed to crowd Beth. The pushing and milling of all the people reminded Beth of her opening night. Panic rose in her throat, "Murphy, please." Beth's voice was barely above a whisper. Above the noise, Murphy did not hear Beth's whisper, but he did turn his head to see how she was faring. Not spotting her, he turned angry eyes backwards trying to spot her in the throng of people. He saw her and started to shout when he also noticed her face.

With quick strides he reached Beth's side, "Beth," Murphy whispered, "What is it, are you all right?"

Beth turned her white face to him, she dropped her bags and clung to him. "Oh, Murphy please help me, get me out of here!" Murphy's arms tightened around her trembling form, he picked up Beth's luggage and tucked his own under his arms. "Hold onto my arm, Beth, I'll get you out. Don't let go." His voice broke through to Beth, it brooked no nonsense and gave her little time to think. Clutching his arm, she followed Murphy outside.

A cold sweat had broken out on Beth's forehead, her legs were weak. "Oh God," Beth murmured, "Not again, not here." Tears willed in her hazel eyes, and slowly trickled down her cheeks.

Setting their luggage down, Murphy took Beth in his arms once more, speaking softly he said, "You're outside now, Beth. I won't let you get hurt; I'll protect you. Do you believe that Beth?" with one hand he raised her chin, blue eyes stared into hazel again, trying to comfort and reassure.

Beth's voice shook as she answered, "Yes, I'm so sorry, silly of me," her voice trailed away. Shielding her with his body from the looks of curious bystanders, Murphy's grasp relaxed a little. Beth regained her composure feeling very secure and safe in his arms. "I'm such a fool," Beth thought. "Murphy must think me an idiot. He's being so nice. Maybe he's human after all." "I'm ok now," Beth whispered, looking up.

Murphy looked at the small heart-shaped face, the two large eyes, the small put nose sprinkled with freckles, and the delicately trembling mouth. Without thinking, he bent his head. In a featherlike kiss his lips gently brushed Beth's. A shock of feeling flooded Beth's body at his touch, startling aware of the magnetism in his presence. Raising his head, Murphy attempted to lighten the heavy atmosphere of the last few minutes, "I never did get to kiss my bride, did I?"

Beth gave a faint grin, "Does that mean the marriage isn't legal and we do this all over again?"

Murphy smiled, "Not on your life, ready to go?"

His question held the hidden thought of whether or not she was capable now of continuing. Beth nodded, very touched by Murphy's tender words. "Ready, Boss."

Together they picked up the cases once more and together they walked to the parking lot. Murphy walked to a dark grey SUV and pulled out the keys. Unlocking the car, he let Beth in and put the cases in the back. Climbing in, his size seemed to fill the car. He had once more become the stranger Beth had married.

Murphy drove with ease onto the busy St. Louis traffic. Neither spoke as they traveled past Forest Park, down Kingshighway to Rt. 40. Mile after mile of high-rise buildings, restaurants, Busch stadium, home of the St. Louis Cardinals. "Had Murphy ever played there," Beth wondered but did not ask. They could see the waterfront now, the mighty Mississippi, and towering above it all the Arch, a 630-foot glistening silver monument to all those settlers and pioneers who had traveled through St. Louis to the far distant land of the west. Crossing now Martin Luther King Bridge, Beth looked down into the muddy waters of the Mississippi.

She watched as barges moved slowly downstream as well as the riverfront paddleboats which catered to the tourists. The "Tom Sawyer" and "Huck Finn" riverboats could also be seen, glistening red, white, and blue in the spring sunshine. Their names made immortal by the writings of Sam Clemens better known as Mark Twain.

Once across the river, the traffic seemed to disappear. Turning onto Interstate 70, Murphy looked at Beth. "Feeling better?" he asked.

Beth took a deep breath, letting it out slowly. "How much do you know about me?"

"Only what Daniels, your uncle told me. I've known him all my life and he's one of the few people I trust." Murphy replied.

"That doesn't tell me what you know," Beth said. "What has he told you about my past?"

"He told me he knew of a girl who would be perfect in mothering my niece and nephew. He told me I could trust you, that you were young, unspoiled and had courage, or rather spunk. He told me if anyone could convince my sister-in-law and help the children it would be you. Like I said, I trust in his judgment and here we are. What more would you like me to know, Beth?"

"Did he mention to you why I would marry you, without meeting you?"

Murphy shook his head, and gave Beth a sideways glance, "You don't have to tell me anything you know. Our pasts are unimportant to our marriage. We shall go from day to day, okay?"

Beth shook her head, "I'd like to explain a little. My parents died when I was sixteen, they were super but rather old fashioned. Girls were supposed to get married

21

not have careers. When they died, I decided I didn't want pity or charity. I did live with Uncle Henry for two years when I finished High School, but I also took voice lessons. I've always been able to sing, and I hoped it would be my ticket to stand on my own two feet. When I graduated, I was able to get a job singing with a group of kids at the local college. We played three or four nights a week. During the day, I started taking college courses. I studied voice and worked part-time to help pay my way. I graduated two years ago and with my graduation I received an offer to start singing with a friend of Uncle Henry's. His name is Johnny Duncan, he's a pianist, a very good one. We arranged our own act, some popular songs, some we wrote ourselves. We played weddings, small discos, anything. A year ago, we had our big break, a small nightclub signed us to appear nightly. On our opening night," Beth paused. Even now she could see the scene again in her eyes, she closed her eyes and swallowed. She started again, "On opening night a fire broke out. Everything happened at once, people were everywhere. Johnny and I were the last to get out. I suffered some damage to my lungs from the smoke. Also, I have scars on my shoulders and back. I spent a lot of time in the hospital, the skin graphs and therapy. My voice is fine, but I can't ever sing for my supper so to say. I freeze whenever I'm around a lot of people. Back at the airport ... all those people ... it was happening all over again... sometimes I can even imagine I smell smoke. I've tried to get a job since in offices and so on, but I get the same feeling, I panic. Right now, my money's gone, I won't sponge off Uncle Henry or Johnny. I look on helping you as helping me, it's a job I might be able to handle." Beth stopped;

Murphy had not said a word through her lengthy monologue. *He's disgusted with me at my cowardice. He's probably blaming Uncle Henry.* Beth swallowed, and without realizing stuck her chin out. "It's not too late to take me back, Murphy. I'll explain to Uncle Henry. I'm sorry," her voice trailed away.

"Like I said before," Murphy began. "I trust your Uncle Henry's judgment."

Beth let out a sigh of relief, "Now about that rundown on the house, the sister-in-law, and the kids," he continued. "First the house and farm, my grandparents owned about 200 acres of bottomland in Elsah. Gramps had an orchard of apples and peaches, raised some Herefords, some chickens, a few pigs, planted about half his fields in corn, the other in wheat. He made a decent living. I can't ever remember doing without anything. Marshall, my brother, and I inherited the farm two years ago when my grandparents died within a few months of each other. The farm's been empty since. It's going to require a lot of work to fix it up, just to make it livable not fancy. I guess Marsh wanted his kids to have the same upbringing we had for his own children. I was given a set amount of money to start things up on the farm, after that we live only on what we make. We can afford some paint and we'll see what furniture we need but the majority of the money needs to go for livestock and our first crops. When the judge goes down with the decision in a year, I want everything down in black and white that we did it just like the will said. It'll be rough but I think we can manage."

Beth nodded and waited for Murphy to continue, "Now for Celia, that's my sister-in-law's name. She hates me and would do anything in her power to see me fall on my face. She is beautiful and intelligent, unfortunately she's also greedy and totally without any sense of morality. How she even had a sister like Joanna is beyond me. She's a model and an actress, you'll recognize her when you see her. Be careful around her, we'll have to act like a normal married couple complete with sharing the same bedroom." At Beth's quick indrawn breath, he hurried on, "I said the same room not bed. If my memory serves me there's a dressing room off the master bedroom, we'll put a day bed in there and that's where I'll sleep. To the outside world including Mike and Jenny we'll be the normal marriage, only we'll know different. I won't take advantage of you Beth, I've had my fill of beautiful women and while I'm not a monk, I'll keep my promise. Do you believe me, Beth?"

Beth hesitated and looked into the same dark blue eyes she had only first seen a few days before. Eyes that had been cold, ruthless, warm and understanding," I trust Uncle Henry's judgement too, Murphy. Yes, I do believe you."

A few moments passed before Murphy continued, "and now the children. I've never seen them; in the last five years I've kept in touch with my brother by phone. They were a close family, I know. I've changed over the years, become a bit cynical, cold I've been told. That's where you come in Beth. Show them love and warmth, make them welcome. I don't know if I can or if I'm even capable of helping them. I'm a bit worried they'll be afraid of me, with the scar and all. I'm sure Celia has told them some very nice bedtime stories about the uncle with the scar that will not want them or some other such drivel." He paused for a breath, with a wry grin he said, "Honeymoon over before it begins. Right? Beth, I'm a rotten person, I'm selfish, I don't really care about anyone else, but I did love my brother and will do my utmost for his kids, including getting married to a stranger and dragging her through hell with living with me and getting the farm back to order. I've got dreams of what the farm can be, of what it was. Have I frightened you off?"

Beth laughed, a golden sound. "If we aren't a pair! Both wondering if we've scared the other off. We'll do okay Murphy. Just wait and see."

Murphy returned Beth's smile, "Daniels was right," he thought, "she is a spunky little thing." Aloud he said, "Friends, Beth?"

Beth's laugh broke again, "Yes, husband, I think we'll be friends!"

No more was said, each content and comfortable as the car moved steadily on. They had reached Alton now, the brick roads reminded of past years, past the tall, towering mills of grain, turning onto the Great River Road, a road that travels side by side along the cliffs of the Mississippi River. Flanked on one side by the cliffs and trees, bare, the green of spring as yet a promise; the other side faced the river, always changing. Here and there one saw sailboats and motorboats. A few barges and tugboats were parked along the wharfs.

"What a beautiful way to travel!" Beth exclaimed. "It's so fresh and clear, so unspoiled."

Murphy agreed, "I'm glad you like it, you'll be traveling along it often enough. Most of your shopping will be done here in Alton, also this is where the hospital is...several as a matter of fact. Elsah's not too far from here, just a few miles north of the Piasa Bird.

"The what?" Beth asked.

"Piasa Bird, it's an old Illini Indian legend. They used to live in these cliffs. Unfortunately, so did this bird, part lizard, dragon, and bird all rolled into one. It would swoop down on the children and warriors of the Illini and carry them off and eat them. One of the chiefs decided he had enough and laid a trap to kill the Piasa Bird. He used himself as bait and stationed his warriors behind the bushes and trees. Sure, enough along came the old devil. Just as he made his big move, the chief threw his spear at the heart of the Bird. All his warriors did the same. Needless to say, he died. In order to scare all other devils from the cliffs, they painted a picture of him on the cliffs. It's been repainted several times since, of course, but the picture is the same. There it is, right to your left."

He swung the car into the lay of grass between the road and cliff. Murphy had done a creditable job of explaining the monster painted. His face was that of a dragon complete with fire out of its mouth, large wings resembling those of a pterodactyl held the body of the large lizard. Huge claws were also in evidence as well as a very strong tail. He was a frightening sight; made even more so by the thought of the towering cliffs he had been painted on.

After several minutes they drove on, turning right into the town of Elsah. Breathing in a delighted gasp at the town unfolding before her eyes, Beth watched in fascination as they drove down narrow brick roads, houses lined both sides complete with the hitching post of an earlier era. It was like stepping back in time.

Flowers had begun to vine and emerge from window boxes and gardens. Shutters were latched from the windows of each house. Built on a hill the town grew upward, past the wooden one-way bridge, with the clear shining stream bubbling below, past the now deserted water wheel that had ground the grain for decades before, past the dogs barking and children playing, past the tiny shops each with their own wooden sign. Beth was enchanted, even more so as Murphy stopped in front of one of the stores.

"Come on," he said, "let's eat." He led her into a narrow entrance foyer of the Country Kitchen and seated themselves at the cozy table, with the yellow and white gingham tablecloth, and the old-fashioned periodic dishes. Still bemused Beth let Murphy order for her, the specialty of the house, freshly caught river buffalo, fried with a hint of lemon, scalloped potatoes, and delicately buttered broccoli, and homemade bread. Beth had forgotten she was hungry, ravenously so. Together they ate in companionable silence. When finished, Murphy deliberately took Beth's hand and kissed the ring that pronounced to the world of their marriage. Beth tried to withdraw her hand, shocked at the touch of electricity that seemed to go through her entire body. She felt as if her hand was burned.

Murphy lowered his head, to an onlooker he seemed to be whispering in her ear. But his voice was not love like, almost hastily he spoke, "We're newlyweds and the sooner this town realizes that, the easier they'll tell Celia if asked. Now stop looking as if I bit you instead of kissed your hand!" His words had only been heard by Beth, and they had the intended effect, with eyes that were sparkled with glints of gold. Beth whispered back,

"Act 1, Scene 2, I take it." She squeezed Murphy's hand and grinned shyly up at him. "Isn't it time we were going dear?" A blush rose traitorously up her cheeks. Making her the typical, eager bride.

Murphy gave the waitress the full extent of his charming smile, "My compliments to a truly special wedding supper. My bride and I will be back, we're taking up the old Whitaker Farm." Again, the smile, he never let go of Beth's hand as he paid the bill, added a generous tip and led Beth out the door to the car.

An unsmiling Murphy now drove on through the picturesque town. He suddenly asked abruptly, "Do you drive?"

"Yes," Beth answered, "I've never owned a car but like all other American children learned at the ripe old age of 16--drivers training, everything. Why?"

Murphy braked. "This car is yours; we're picking up my truck here. Follow my lead, okay?"

Beth nodded; a bit confused. The drive had been pleasant enough and now Murphy had reverted back to the cold man she had first seen. Sighing, she scooted over the seat and adjusted the pedals to her legs instead of the long ones of Murphy. Looking up it was to see him talking to another man, she saw the exchange of money for what she supposed were keys. Murphy turned, walked over to a fairly new black pickup. He caught her gaze and signaled to her to follow him. Backing up and following the truck along the country roads took all Beth's concentration, although she did take careful note of how to get back to Elsah and in time turn onto the highway to Alton. At last Murphy signaled he was turning, and Beth followed, seeing her new home for the first time.

CHAPTER 3

The lane which they drove was lined on either side by a wood fence, crisscrossing down the lane and on the bordering road. The paint was peeling, and in several places, boards were missing. The lane itself needs work, thought Beth, as she narrowly missed another pothole. Weeds were knee deep everywhere even in the early days of spring. It needed a lot of time and care, yet with overwhelming work staring at her, Beth was impressed. There was the house behind the huge trees, a two-story country cottage. At one time it must have been white, a few of the shutters hanging by a few nails. From the windows, Beth thought probably four bedrooms up, four rooms down. The back porch where Murphy was parking was screened--partially at least, great gaps were in evidence. The yard was enormous and at one time must have been his grandmother's pride and joy. There were flowering bushes and the beginnings of roses and lilacs. A few flowering trees were scattered in the yard, as well as a massive willow to the back and several evergreen bushes against the house. About 50 feet from the back door was a cluster of buildings, Beth thought the small one with the partially fenced yard was probably used for chickens. The barn was large, but the paint had long since disappeared, the huge double door hung by a single hinge. Other shapes could be seen in the darkening twilight. Probably storage sheds, Beth thought. She climbed out of the car and turned to face Murphy.

Murphy's look was grim as he surveyed his surroundings with a very critical eye. Without even turning to face Beth, he said, "It's a mess, any suggestions as to where to start?"

Beth raised one eye and said impishly, "How about a place to sleep? We'll look everything over in the morning and make a list of priorities. Who knows, it might not look so discouraging in the fresh light of the early morn!"

Murphy's surprised look and sheepish grin had Beth laughing in full force. "Thought I'd turn tail and run?" Beth asked.

"I wouldn't have blamed you if you had. I had no idea how run-down things were. The lawyer said it was in pretty good shape."

Beth interrupted, "Sounds like the kind of lawyer to have if you'd ever committed a crime. I can hear him now, they're dead, but they're in good shape!" She had managed to lighten Murphy's mood as she saw him grin.

"Let's check out the house, see if it's safe to sleep there or better to camp down in the wagon." He took hold of Beth's hand to help her over the uneven grass to the back door. He pushed in the screen latch and it fell slowly back, squeaking as it opened. Walking across the floor littered with dirt and leaves, Beth tried not to think of what else. Murphy used a key to open the back door. It opened into the kitchen, cobwebs barred their entrance and Murphy impatiently knocked them down as he led the way into the large shadowy room. Wooden cabinets lined two entire sides of the room. The doors were on other walls of the room; pushing one open, Beth discovered it to be a pantry with shelves going up both sides of its walls. The other led to a storage room...looks like there might be room for a washer and dryer and freezer, Beth thought. The third led into the dining room where the once pretty wallpaper now lay faded and peeling on the floor. The dining room led to the living room. A fireplace lined one wall of the room. The staircase was open on one side and split the living and dining room. On the far side of the living room was another door, Beth carefully opened it. Book lined shelves lined two walls of the den, as well as paneled walls in a very dusty shade of maple. Beth turned as Murphy started up the stairs, she hurried after him as he walked slowly up the winding staircase. At the top there was a long hallway with six doors, three on each side. Murphy pushed open the first, it revealed a large bedroom. The second was to a bathroom, the third to another bedroom. The other side contained two more bedrooms and a large linen closet.

Murphy talked more to himself than Beth as he noted that at least the roof was in fairly good shape, there seemed no evidence of leaks and all the windows were intact. "A good cleaning, some paint--not too bad," he said. Turning to her he asked, "In or out?"

"Outside," Beth answered, "I have the opinion we're not alone in this house and until I clean it and get rid of all unwelcome visitors I'm sleeping in the car!"

Grinning devilishly, Murphy agreed and together they went down the stairs and back outside. "I'll get the electricity, gas, water and phone hooked up tomorrow. Let's unload the truck and then we'll hit the sack, okay?"

Beth nodded numbly, exhaustion from the day, together with the tension of the airport, the long drive and arrival finally hit her full force. She stumbled on the way; Murphy's hands gripped her quickly about the waist. Beth drew her breath in sharply, alarmingly aware of the overwhelming maleness of Murphy. His broad muscular shoulders, his hands, large and powerful. Beth felt suddenly very small, and very vulnerable. Alone on the farm with this disturbingly handsome stranger, what's to keep him from hurting me, doing whatever he wants. Beth could envision his strong arms holding her, his lean arrogant face coming closer to hers, his mouth hard, demanding on hers. Beth felt herself tremble uncontrollably in Murphy's hands. She looked up at his features in the dim light of the twilight.

Murphy repeated himself, "Beth are you alright? Beth?" He gave her a slight shake. Numbly Beth looked at Murphy, she shook her head, for the moment unable to speak. His features softened for a moment, "You're all in. We'll finish this in the morning. Let's get the sleeping bags and get settled."

He led Beth to the car, he took out their luggage placing it in the truck. He carried two sleeping bags back with him. He leaned into the wagon and put the back seat down. He carefully spread the sleeping bags out. Turning to Beth, he bowed low and murmured, "The honeymoon suite awaits, madam."

Beth grinned back, touched at his attempt to relieve her of the apprehension she had felt only a few moments earlier. "How romantic, it's perfect, Murphy. You do think of everything!"

They settled themselves into the sleeping bags, keeping the rear window of the station wagon open. Beth had never been in such close sleeping quarters before. Murphy seemed to fill the wagon. She rolled to the farthest side, trying to give him as much room as possible. Looking up through the open window, Beth noticed how clear the sky seemed, how bright the stars twinkled. They were her last thought as sleep finally caught up with her and her eyes slowly closed in slumber. She was unaware of being covered by her sleeping bag, or of a large hand gently wiping the lonely tears which fell across her cheek. Unaware of the dark eyes which looked at her and noticed again how clear her skin was, the heart shape of her face, and the lips, soft and inviting even in sleep.

"She reminds me," Murphy thought, "of the angel that used to hang above my bed when I was small. We shall see, we shall see ..."

Sleep at least claimed Murphy, too.

Beth awoke to the chirping of birds and the first rays of sun were slowly showing over the trees. A mist seemed suspended over the fields and the dew sparkled in the grass like glistening diamonds. Beth slowly turned so as not to wake the sleeping form beside her. Looking at Murphy relaxed, his face seemed years younger. The harsh lines around his mouth and eyes were gone. He looked like a little boy. Even his scar seemed to fade.

Moving slowly Beth crept out of her bag and through the open car window. Outside she stretched, and taking her small suitcase, brushed her hair and freshened up, changing into clean, well-worn jeans and a yellow knit tee-shirt. Walking over to the truck, she looked in the back surprised at the gear that had been loaded. "Coffee," she decided, and taking out the Coleman camp stove and coffee pot proceeded to make just that. "What else do we have here," she mused and started looking through the boxes of food.

Murphy stretched and hit his arm on the wagon roof. Memory came back. Oh yes, back at the old homestead. Gran must be cooking breakfast; I can smell the coffee. Suddenly his eyes were wide awake, Gran was dead. Beth ... he turned to look at her empty side. She couldn't be, he thought and climbed out of the wagon. Walking over to the truck, his hair still tousled from sleep, he looked in amazement at the sight of Beth working at the camp stove. Hearing him approach Beth called over her shoulder, "Morning, sleepyhead. How does some coffee sound? I hope you don't mind but I also decided to cook up some bacon and eggs I found, okay?" She turned when Murphy made no attempt at answering her. She saw his look of amazement and her chuckle came from deep within her throat. "Wake up, Murphy. It's no dream. I really am cooking breakfast!"

"I don't believe it," he said. "I figured you'd sleep till noon and I'd have to bring you coffee!" He shook his head, "Are you for real?"

"Find us a seat and see for yourself," Beth quipped. "If my food doesn't wake you up, this coffee will. I think it's strong enough to walk by itself!"

Murphy grinned and walked to the tailgate of the truck. He lowered it and reached in for two camp stools inside. Placing them side by side, he again turned to Beth. "All set, Boss," he quipped.

"Not yet," Beth said and reaching into the box nearest her, she spread out a colored scarf to act as a tablecloth. She placed salt and pepper and cups of coffee down. Then she placed the silverware. Going back to the stove she heaped two plates with bacon and eggs and toast and carried them to their makeshift table. Seating herself, she said, "Now, we're set!"

Murphy sat beside her, shaking his head. "You are full of surprises Beth, pleasant one's mind you, but surprises all the same!" He started to eat but was stopped as Beth folded her hands and said a simple blessing before the meal. Making the sign of the cross, she touched Murphy's arm, "I didn't mean to stop you from eating, it's safe. You can dig in."

Murphy continued looking at Beth, abruptly he said, "I didn't know you were religious, or even Catholic."

"All my life," she said, "that's one reason why I didn't mind the register's office. I'm not really married in my mind, so when we separate it won't be any problem in the eyes of the church."

For a reason unknown to Murphy, the thought that Beth didn't really feel married to him, rankled. "But we really are married," he spoke quietly.

Beth nodded, "By law, yes, but not by the church, I wouldn't even feel really married unless it was by a priest." Looking up, she smiled, "How's the breakfast?"

"Fine," Murphy mumbled, and tackled his breakfast, thinking what a strange girl he had married. When finished, he stood up. "I'm going into town to see about the water, electricity, gas and telephone. Anything you want? Or would you like to ride along?"

Beth gave him an impish grin. "Well, since there's not much to do around here, I'll come along. I need some cleaning supplies if we're going to make this house livable!"

Later after shopping and turning on all utilities, they headed back to the farm. Once there, Murphy and Beth tackled the kitchen together. They washed down walls and scrubbed the floor. Beth washed down the cabinets and cleaned them out. Then Murphy tackled the bathroom, making sure they could at least use the toilet and shower.

When they finished, it was growing dark and they both grinned as Murphy switched on the lamp.

"Let there be light," Beth quipped.

Murphy returned the quip with a deep chuckle. "Not a bad day's work. We can sleep on the floor in the kitchen. We have running water. I won't feel so bad now about leaving tomorrow."

All afternoon their easy working relationship had led to their talking of both parties about their lives, their likes and dislikes, their tastes of music and poetry. They had talked of everything yet nothing of his absence on the morrow.

His words fell like a bombshell to Beth's ears. "You're leaving?" Beth asked.

"I'm sorry, I hate leaving you by yourself, but I need to purchase the livestock to make this farm a working proposition. I also need to see the lawyer and set the paperwork in motion, not to mention some loose ends I need to tie up."

"How long will you be gone?" Beth murmured.

"About two weeks, give or take a few days. No longer than is necessary, I assure you. You don't feel up to staying by yourself?" Dark blue eyes assessed the pale face of Beth.

"No, I'll be fine," pulling herself together Beth said. "Who knows, maybe I'll get so much done you won't recognize the place!"

"You'll be so busy, you won't even know I'm gone," Murphy replied. Beth smiled as she was expected to but thinking at the same time how very lonely it would be, already missing this stranger who was her husband.

CHAPTER 4

Murphy left first thing in the morning, having spent a very business-type evening with Beth. No smiles crossed his face, no laughter, just the old, cold arrogant man she had first met. Beth thought with a touch of wistfulness, already missing those few times she had glimpsed a very different person. Beth sighed, "Well, best get to work. It definitely won't get done without both of us!"

Since Murphy left, it was time to see room by room what furniture was there, what was usable and what they would need to buy. She also measured for drapes and curtains. She fixed a sandwich for lunch and decided to walk around the farm. Maybe get a feeling for what it had been or should be again.

She crossed the barnyard, looking little more than a teenager in her faded jeans, plaid shirt and sweater, her hair pulled back with a ribbon. With lithe, long even strides she soon had reached the first gate and then another. The fields were just starting to turn green, the trees showed buds and the promise of summer shade. The crisp, cool spring morning suddenly didn't look so lonely.

A wisp of smoke caught Beth's eye coming from beyond the orchard. "Look at all those lovely trees, Beth thought, they certainly don't look like they've been neglected for two years. They're freshly pruned and trimmed. I wonder who? Maybe the smoke will be my explanation. She stopped as she heard someone calling.

"Hello. You! Wait up!"

Beth froze. Alone in the orchard, knowing no one, she felt very vulnerable. She turned and watched a tall shape hurry closer. Beth took a closer look as the shape took the form of a man dressed in black and wearing, Beth looked again, and smiled, a clerical collar! "Hello, Father," Beth spoke. "I hardly expected to see anyone here!"

The priest grinned and offered his hand to Beth, "Good morning, my child." His voice had a soft Scottish sound. "Are your parents the new owners of these lovely trees?"

"My parents?" Beth was puzzled.

"Well yes, we heard Mr. Whitaker's grandson had come with his children to farm the old homestead. We're delighted to have someone living there again. An empty house is so sad. An empty farm doubly so."

"Father," Beth spoke quietly, "your information is correct but it's not my parents, it's my husband and me. The children are our niece and nephew. Their parents were recently killed."

"Oh, I am so sorry," the priest answered. "You're but a child yourself!"

"Not much younger than yourself Father," Beth impishly answered taking in the lean lines of this youthful looking priest, his wavy brown hair, the gray eyes behind the glasses he wore, the strong square chin.

"Well," the priest blushed, "maybe not but old enough to be your 'father' all the same!" he grinned. "Let me introduce myself, Father John MacNair, called Father Mac by my parishioners at St. Mary's. We're located just over that hill. Welcome to the community, Mrs. Whitaker."

"Beth, Elizabeth really, but I'd like you to call me Beth. Is St. Mary's a large parish, Father?"

"No, only about 400 families. We're small enough to get involved in everyone else's business, but large enough not to make it too often! We do have a school, about 150 kids, 8 classrooms. We have three Dominican sisters to help teach and run things plus five lay teachers. Because we're small we don't have a lot of money. Things cost the same but like everybody else we are always looking for ways to raise money. That's er...why I was hoping to see Mr. Whitaker." Suddenly Father Mac looked nervous.

Beth smiled, a lazy smile that started in her eyes and spread to the dimple in her left cheek. "Father Mac, Murphy, Mr. Whitaker, will not be back for two weeks. Suppose you tell me what's on your mind. It's bound to be important to have you coming to see us the second day we arrive. I won't bite, Father, and maybe we... I can help?" Beth touched his arm and smiled.

Father MacNair smiled ruefully. "Don't be trying any of that Irish charm on me young lady. You don't need it! I'll be glad to talk to you. I'm sure you're much prettier, anyhow."

Beth gave an answering chuckle. "How on earth did you know I was Irish, Father?"

"Well, I had my first hint with the emerald eyes and the small scattering of sun kissed freckles on your nose. Then when I heard your name, I was sure. Elizabeth is an Irish name. But the clincher was the charm you have, no one but an Irish lass would try and flirt with an old priest such as me."

40

"Father, would you by any chance have kissed the Blarney stone yourself?" Beth queried.

"Well, as a matter of fact, my mother, God rest her soul, was Irish. Dad was Scottish."

"Does that make you a thrifty charmer, Father?" Beth asked jokingly. Together they laughed.

"Okay, Father, what is the problem you need to see Murphy about?" Beth sat down on the soft turf under one of the trees. She motioned for the priest to join her. "Okay Father, shoot. You talk and I'll listen." She turned trusting eyes on the man and waited.

Father Mac looked around at the orchard, leaned back against the trunk of the tree and began his story. "When I came to Elsah as a young priest some ten years ago, we had a church, nothing more. I started a youth group and eventually we decided a school was in order. Buildings cost money and money was something not many people around here have much of, not many go hungry mind you, but there's never enough left over. We took to having raffles and Bingo. The money grew slowly. Then one day I had a visitor. Someone I had met but didn't really know. He introduced himself as Matthew Whitaker. He said he had heard I had a dream with a problem. He wondered if he helped me would I in turn help him, for it seemed he too had a problem with his dream. His dream he told me was to keep his farm going as a working farm even though he was getting on in years. He mentioned he had some grandsons who he wanted to one day hand over the farm to. Not a rundown headache but a thriving business, something to pass on from one generation to another. He was getting old, he explained, and things were going undone. He had a hired hand, but he wasn't able to do everything. The gist

41

of the message was...would we take over working on the farm for pay. Not everything, mainly the orchard. If we kept it trimmed and pruned and picked the first fruit, we got a set amount per hour worked plus the going rate for picking. He got the profit from the sale of the fruit, apples and peaches. From the sale of the fruit, he gave an additional gift to the school building fund. It may not sound like much, but almost by this task alone we built our school and paid for it. Two years ago, our friend Matthew Whitaker died. We waited for those grandsons to come and they didn't. The trees had become a part of us by then, we just couldn't let the fruit rot on the ground or let the plants go to seed. I'm not trying to justify what we've done, just explain why." Father Mac stopped for breath and ran his hand through his hair.

Beth spoke softly, "Over the last two years, you've continued nurturing and caring for your friend's orchard, haven't you, Father?"

"Yes, we continued the original arrangement, paying the hourly rate and then our picking time, but the rest we put in an account at the bank. It's there now for you and your husband. I don't know what arrangements you'll be making but if you need someone, we'd like to apply for the job."

"How much money is in the bank, Father?" Beth questioned.

"Almost $20,000," he replied.

Beth's astonishment at the amount was evident. "That's an awful lot of money, Father. Thank you for telling me. We can certainly use the money in getting the farm started up again." They stood up and she held out her hand. "I'd like to come visit you, Father."

"Aye, child, I'd like that." With that Father Mac started back the way he had come, through the trees of apples and peaches to the faraway steps of St. Mary's.

Beth watched him go. "Murphy can certainly use that money," she thought, there were so many things that needed doing and none of them being done while I'm out here." She noticed again the smoke rising from over the hill. "Why not," she mused, "I've lost most the afternoon anyway!"

She continued walking toward the hill. I should have asked Father Mac who lives here, she mused as she trudged on, it would certainly have saved my feet a few steps! Her thoughts were interrupted by the barking of a dog as she walked into the clearing that surrounded the tiny hut. It looked little more than a lean-to with a chimney. The dog continued barking and then growled as Beth kept walking. She began talking in a low even voice, almost singing a lullaby to calm the dog. The dog stopped growling as he kept his watchful eyes on Beth's slow-moving form corning closer. Slowing, moving only an inch at a time, Beth's hand came out and touched the dog's head. She kept on the steady monologue to the dog, "Easy, boy, I won't hurt you. Is anybody home? ...Good boy ..."

The dog finally gave a last growl, turned and lay down in the shade. Beth walked to the front door and knocked tentatively at first, then louder as there was no response. "Hello," Beth called out. Beth listened closely. Was that a moan she heard? She turned the handle on the door. It opened slowly. Beth called again, "Hello. Is anyone here?" This time Beth heard a definite moan. She glanced toward the sound in the darkened room. The one room hut was very clean. To the right were a

43

table and shelves, a pot-bellied stove occupied the center of the room and to the left was a bunk. The moan came from the bed. Instinctively Beth moved to that moan. Lying in the bed under some very old quilts was a wizened, whiskered gnome of a man. His flushed face gave Beth the answer to why he moaned. He was burning up with fever. Walking to the stove Beth took a pot of water off. It was boiling now and had been for some time. On the table lay some tea. Beth made a weak tea laced with sugar. Walking to the bed, she held the cup to his dry parched lips. The man opened his eyes and saw a small heart shaped face. "Drink this," a soft voice whispered. The man drank thirstily then slipped back into a deep sleep. He needs help, Beth decided, but I can't leave him for long. Let's see what he's got here and then we'll tackle the problem of help. She found some soup and heated it up on the stove, also a half-used bottle of aspirin.

Again, she stirred the sleeping form, coaxed him into taking the aspirin and soup and let him fall asleep again. With cool water, she sponged his face and hands. He felt a little cooler. Maybe now Beth could go and get help. She slipped out the door, gave the dog some water and leftover soup and started walking quickly back towards the orchard. Father Mac said his church adjoined the orchard, so I'll look in the direction he had walked, Beth reasoned. That way! She started running now, calling out as she ran. "Father Mac, Father Mac!" She saw the outline of the buildings nestled amongst the trees. At the door of the church, Beth paused to get her breath. She walked into the cool stone walls. A gasp of pleasure escaped her lips at the beautiful interior. The building was built entirely of rough white stone. The

Stations of the Cross which hung on both sides of the walls were made of dark wood, sculptured with loving hands to show the pain and agony of Christ. The altar was again of white stone and marble, the crucifix behind the altar, again the dark wood. Beth touched the holy water, made the sign of the cross with trembling fingers. She drew her eyes from the lovely sacristy of the church and continued looking for Father Mac. Perhaps he's in the room where he would keep his vestments preparing for evening mass, Beth hoped, and walked up the center aisle towards the door leading off the altar. She knelt briefly at its base, and hurried on, knocking softly at the door. She heard the sound of footsteps, "Thank you, God," she whispered. The door opened by a young boy dressed in his altar white cloth. Beth did not wait for him to speak. "Father Mac, please, it's an emergency."

She saw a dark figure approaching, "What is it, David?" Then noticing the figure standing in the doorway, "Why Beth, child, what's wrong?"

"Father... there's a hut on the other side of the orchard, a little man ... he's very sick. Can you send a doctor, please? I must get back, he's all alone," Beth turned to go hearing Father already giving the blessed words of help.

"David, call Dr. Williams, tell him to go to Casey's immediately."

Beth retraced her steps. Her side was hurting her from exertion, her breath coming in gasps. She neared the clearing. This time there was no growl to welcome her. The dog recognizing her gave a playful wag of his tail. Beth put a hand on his head and opened the door up quietly, hoping not to disturb Casey as he slept. She felt his head, again washing down his forehead and hands, forcing more of the tea down his parched lips. Again, he opened his eyes, memory came of the heart-shaped face he had seen earlier.

His voice cracked, "Are you an angel?"

Beth smiled and whispered back, "Only if you're really a leprechaun?" Casey smiled, a crooked smile at best and slipped back into sleep again.

Some moments later, Beth was warned of people approaching. Strangers by the warning bark of the dog. She looked out recognizing the form of Father Mac. The other man was unfamiliar but the bag he carried definitely was welcome. "Down, boy," Beth instructed the dog. The dog obeyed and lay down again by the door. Father Mac stopped in astonishment. "I've never seen Bingo obey anyone but old Casey before."

"He probably senses I'm trying to help. Come in, please." The two men followed her into the darkened room. Dr. Williams hurried over to the bed and bent down talking gently to the still form. The two gray heads talked softly to each other as Dr. Williams finished his examination. He chuckled once at something Casey had said and turned to the waiting people on the other side of the room. He was smiling as he joined them, looking appreciatively at the young girl standing beside Father Mac.

He smiled, "He'll be okay. He's too crusty an old codger to be sick for long. I'll give him an injection of penicillin to help knock the infection. He'll need someone to take care of him, he'll never consent to a hospital."

Beth spoke up, "Could he be moved to the house?" The doctor nodded. "Then I'll take care of him. Bingo can come too, there is plenty of room and I can take care of him in between getting the house ready. Will that be okay, Dr. Williams?"

Dr. Williams smiled, "Casey was right. He told me to go home, there was an angel floating around here. He'd like her back ... she was much prettier than I am! I'll leave you medicine for him and check on him every couple of days. We'll also move him for you, right Mac?"

"Right, Don," Father Mac spoke, "Thank you Beth. Casey is a good soul, a bit on the solitary side, he doesn't suffer fools much, says what he thinks. He worked for Matt Whitaker for years. He just couldn't bring himself to leave after he passed on. Maybe he could find some work to do for young Murphy?"

Beth walked to the bed. She knelt down, kissed the weathered cheek, "We're going home Casey, to the Whitaker house. I'm Beth Whitaker. I married Murphy. Will you come home with me, Casey? When you're well, we'd like you to work for us. We need you, Casey. Please say you'll come ...Bingo, too?"

Beth waited. She watched while Casey's pale blue eyes looked at her, seemingly through to her very soul. "Aye, lass, I'll come." A tear rolled down his cheek, "I'll come home."

Beth raised her lovely eyes to the two men standing beside the bed. "We're ready to go. Casey and I are going home."

Only later, after Casey was settled by the fire and Bingo stretched out beside him did Beth wonder at Murphy's reaction to her decision for Casey. Thinking back on the day, Beth decided she really hadn't got much done, but tomorrow she could work again. "At least now we have money," Beth thought, "to fix up the house and farm."

Suddenly Beth sat up in her sleeping bag. Father needs money, he wants to work. Why not let the parish help put this place in order. We can all paint and clean. The money's there. She got up, checked on Casey and walked to the phone. She pushed the correct numbers on the key pad, "Uncle Henry, this is Beth. I'm fine. I have a legal question for you. If money was made on the farm two years ago and was just now turned over, could we use it to fix up the farm without violating our chances for Murphy's niece and nephew?"

Beth listened and smiled, "Thanks, Uncle Henry, I love you too."

Once more she picked up the phone. This time she called the operator to connect the number for her. "Father Mac, this is Beth. No, everything is fine. Were you serious about wanting to work on the orchard? What about the farm? Well, I do have a proposition for you. I need help in fixing up the farm. I want to surprise Murphy. Painting, cleaning, a few repairs...curtains, furniture. We'll pay your parish to help, women too. By the hour, per person. Can it be done in two weeks, Father?... Starting tomorrow morning?... Great, thanks Father. See you at 9:00 tomorrow."

Putting down the phone Beth smiled. She remembered her words to Murphy. 'You might not even recognize the place.' She settled down to sleep. There would be lots to do in the morning.

CHAPTER 5

The next morning dawned bright and sunny and Beth rose early to check on Casey. His fever was down, and his sleep was much lighter. Beth jumped when the phone rang. Hoping the noise wouldn't waken Casey, she hurried to the telephone and picked it up. "Murphy?" she whispered.

"Who else were you expecting?"

"No one," Beth murmured, "I just am not used to hearing the phone ring. It's so quiet here it sounds like a three-piece band when it rings, especially when you're not quite with it yet."

"I guess so," Murphy answered. "I just called to check how you were doing. I rang yesterday but didn't get anybody."

"I went for a walk to the orchard. I met the priest, a Father Mac. Do you remember him, Murphy?" asked Beth.

"Vaguely, I remember my grandfather talking about him sometimes. Why?" Murphy asked gruffly.

"His church has been working the orchards. He gave me some money from the last two years. Can I spend it on fixing up the house? Or do we need it for livestock or such?" Beth's voice dwindled away. He sounded so remote and distant on the phone.

"Fine," Murphy answered. "It can't be much ... "

Beth interrupted, "How have things been going for you? How was your trip? When will you be returning?"

For the first time, Beth thought she detected a note of warmth in his voice, "Miss me already? Or do you just need somebody to carryall the heavy stuff around?"

Beth laughed, "A bit of both actually!"

She heard Murphy's laugh in return, "I'll be in touch. Here's a number where you can reach me. Take care, Beth. See you in two weeks."

"By, Murphy. Take care," Beth whispered back not sure if Murphy even heard them before the line went click. She turned with a light step to arrange the work for the day.

Murphy heard the whispered words, and long after the line went dead, he held the phone in his hand. She's such a strange girl, he thought. Not at all like the kind of girl I'm used to. She seems genuinely caring. Slowly the mask returned to Murphy's face. He remembered other times and other women who had seemed to care. Women only want things, not me, he thought viciously, then softened as he saw hazel eyes. She doesn't know, Murphy, a voice kept saying, be fair, she could be different. Murphy shook his head to clear it. Time will tell, he thought, time will tell.

At 9:00 promptly, Father Mac arrived with about 20 people of all ages. "We're here, Beth, tell us what you want done and we'll begin. I've already written down names and times so we can keep the hourly rate straight. And thanks, Beth, this work makes all the difference to the school," Father Mac said.

"And to us, Father," Beth gave her slow smile. "We need to divide into groups, one for the barn, one for the outer buildings, and one for the house, outside and inside. First, we clean, repair and scrape. Then we start painting. You're all more aware of how things looked before and that's what I want back again.

"There's some furniture upstairs that needs to be aired and then we'll see what we still need. This evening I'm going to order paint and material so from each group I'll need a list of things you'll need to complete the job. We'll break for lunch at 12:00. I've called the Country Kitchen and dinner is coming then for all of us, okay? Father, you know these people, why don't you divide them up?"

The work was tedious as each group started scrubbing and cleaning. The sound of hammers and laughter intermingled as each group went wholeheartedly to their task. By noon, they were more than ready to eat the sandwiches provided. Beth gathered the lists from each of the groups, asking questions as she glanced over each only seeking specific qualifications for each of their needs. When she had finished, she asked more questions as to the best place to get the materials they needed.

Beth looked at the lists. "I don't think I can haul all this in the wagon, and then there's Casey. His fever is down but he's been sleeping all morning. I don't want to leave him alone." Beth turned the thoughts over in her mind wondering what the best course of action would be. Wishing that Murphy were here to make the decisions for her. Murphy, the thought of his reaction to coming home and finding everything done made Beth smile. "Keep going, girl, it'll be worth it just watching his face."

"Father Mac," Beth called, "I need some help." Together they sat on the steps of the porch. Beth gave him the combined list of materials they needed just for fixing things up. Then she gave him a list of materials they were going to need for the house, including drapes and wallpaper. "Now comes the hard part, Father, I also need some appliances, a washer, dryer, freezer, refrigerator, to start with. If I could get them now, I might even add a dishwasher. We've gone over furniture. We're pretty well set for that except a few odd pieces. I don't even know where to go to look for those and I don't want to leave Casey all that long. Any suggestions?"

Father Mac looked at the lists. He leaned back, took off his glasses and cleaned them. "You don't mind used, in good condition?" he asked.

"No, what have you got in mind?"

"We can send Joe Mortland for the paint and repairs in his truck, he'll know more what to get than we will, and he'll probably be able to get a discount. He's a contractor by trade. He can pay. You can settle up with him later."

Beth nodded and Father Mac continued, "There's a small store in town where you can buy your wallpaper, drapery material, paint for the inside. You look through their books and decide what you want, and they'll have it by the next day. Probably deliver it, too. Called the "Etcetera", fancy name for a store that does a little of everything."

Again, Beth nodded, "It sounds perfect, especially as its close. I won't have to leave Casey very long." Beth looked at Father Mac shrewdly. "I can also tell you have something in mind for the used appliances, so tell me. Patience is not one of my virtues!"

Father Mac laughed, "There's a woman of the parish. Her name is Miss Lucy Donovan. She's quite a character. She never married but raised her sister's five children when their ma died in childbirth. She's about 80 now and she's decided she is too old to live by herself. There was a fight among the kids, they all wanted Miss Lucy to stay with them. Miss Lucy being Miss Lucy decided she'd spend some time with each and would settle where she would be happiest and cause the least trouble."

"She sounds like quite a lady," Beth murmured, already picturing a white-haired matriarch quietly rocking in a chair.

"Well, she has a house full of furniture, but she insists only on selling to someone who will treat it right. She may or may not sell it to you."

Beth thought a while, "Well it's worth a try, Father. What have we got to lose?" She paused. "You will go with me, won't you?"

"Sure," he grinned, "I always feel like the Romans throwing Christians to the lions going but I'll go."

Beth chuckled, "Let me check again on Casey and then we'll get Joe going. We'll take off while someone is still here to stay with Casey, okay?"

"You check on Casey. I'll get Joe started. I'll meet you by your car, okay?" Beth nodded and was off. She walked quietly into the kitchen, took some soup down and heated it up on the camp burner. Add a stove, too, Beth thought. She carried it over to Casey and lifting it up to his lips, coaxed him to drink. She then gave him his medicine, set a tall drink by his bed, covered the again sleeping form and tiptoed out again. Seeing Mrs. McCormick in the hall, Beth asked if she would check on

Casey for her. Mrs. McCormick nodded and smiled as Beth bounced off. She thought as the other people working thought, what a lovely young girl she was, a fitting granddaughter for Matt Whitaker to have.

Beth found Father Mac waiting at the car. Joe Mortland's truck already disappearing down the lane. "First to 'Etcetera', that way I can give Miss Lucy a call and time to prepare for our arrival."

Beth drove, familiarizing herself with the car and her new town. 'Etcetera' was a small building but seemed to hold the promise of finding whatever you wanted. Cindy and Jim Campbell were the owners and Beth liked the red haired, freckled faces of the brother and sister at once. Explaining why she had come and introducing themselves at the same time, Cindy pulled out three enormous books. "These two are wallpaper samples, this one is drapery material. Jim, pullout that paint sample sheet we have. Now," Cindy went on, "you can put them together and decide exactly what you'll see in your house."

Father Mac joined Jim in a cup of coffee while Beth made her choices. "I like the country prints, calicos and ginghams. This yellow for the kitchen, three rolls I think, with this cream color paint and these curtains. A heavier material for the drapes, living room and dining room, I like this blue, using a contrasting lighter shade for the walls. Murphy's den in cream, the walls are paneled, no paint but we'll put some green and cream pillows to liven it up a little. The hallway in this country print, it's real old fashioned but its muted color will make a good entrance to any of the rooms. Mike's room in red, white and blue. This will be perfect," she said, pointing to tiny airplanes, trains and buses. "Jenny's room in pink and green, ruffles and flowers. This one," she said pointing to a strawberry shortcake pattern of pink flowers on a cream background with delicate pale green leaves. "The guest room I want in celery green, this one should be alright. Now for the master bedroom, I want a patchwork effect, browns and rust, brick red, burnt orange," she turned a few pages. "Here, this is what I want. Now the bathroom. This calico floral in brown, gold and yellow. Beth looked up, "Did I go too fast?"

Cindy grinned, "Boy, you sure know what you want don't you? What fabulous taste. None of that silk and satin stuff for you! I got it all down. We'll get it and deliver it by...let's see 3:00 tomorrow, okay?"

Beth returned the grin, "Thanks, Cindy, you are a lifesaver."

Cindy replied, "Part of the service, love! Now with the work done I can ask a question that's driving me crazy. Are you really married to the Murphy Whitaker, that gorgeous hunk who played football for the L.A. Trojans?"

"Yes, I am," Beth said, "Do you know Murphy?"

"Yes and no," Cindy replied with a grimace. "He was older than me by a good five years, closer to Jim than anybody else. He always had girls falling all over him, but he had this wall around him. None of them ever got close. We all thought he was crazy leaving the farm to play football, especially when Marshall didn't even like farming, but I guess you already know when Murphy makes up his mind nobody's going to change it."

Beth grinned. "I had noticed," she said. "Do many of the people around here know Murphy?"

"I'm sure they know of him, but I don't think anyone really knew Murphy. He was sort of the black sheep of the family so to speak. Personally, I think he made things as bad as they were to make Marshall feel better."

"What do you mean, Cindy? I've never met Marshall. We were married after the accident. But I do know that Murphy loved his brother very much." Who else would marry a stranger, she thought!

"You know what a hunk Murphy is, right? Well, Marshall was nothing like him. He was only about 5'10" and he was a lot slighter. Murphy always fought his battles and Murphy being as large as he was came off looking like a definite bully. Sometimes I think Marshall would start things just so Murphy could finish them, the result being Murphy was blamed for what Marshall did."

"What about his grandparents? Didn't they see what was going on?" Beth interrupted.

"They sure did. Old Matt was a lot like Murphy and the two of them were very close. That was part of the problem, too. Marshall was very jealous of Murphy. Can you imagine living in Murphy's shadow? He did everything well, sports, grades, girls and he was terrific on the farm," Cindy said reflectively.

"Why did he leave, Cindy?" Beth asked. At Cindy's questioning look, Beth added, "he doesn't talk much about his family."

"That I can understand," Cindy nodded. "Nobody really knows for sure. A rumor went around that he had gotten a girl in trouble. Matt told him to get married. Murphy said he'd never marry unless he loved her. He left. He never came back. We read about him, of course, on the field and off. Marshall left too, shortly after

56

Murphy. Matt never mentioned either of the boys although I don't think he ever stopped thinking about them, Murphy especially."

"You said it was rumored. You don't really believe that, do you?" Beth felt as if she had to know the answer.

"No, Jim says Murphy left because Marshall would never have a chance unless he did. The girl was just a rumor. No names were ever given. I don't think she ever existed. Murphy was never a saint and I doubt ever celibate, sorry about that. I forget you're married to him," Cindy broke off clearly embarrassed.

"No harm done. I do appreciate the information," Beth assured her, feeling slightly guilty for having encouraged the girl's confidence. "Father," she raised her voice, "are you ready to leave to go Miss Lucy's?"

"Yes, we'll have to hurry if we don't want to keep her waiting. Thanks Jim, Cindy. See you in Mass," he held the door and out they hurried.

Father Mac directed Beth to a quaint little house about three streets over. Walking up the steps to the house, Beth thought back to her conversation with Cindy. Will I ever understand the coldness in your eyes, Murphy? Will I ever be able to pass beyond the barrier you've built? Take care girl, she chided. It's only for one year, no strings remember. To break down that wall would be a commitment forever.

They rang the doorbell. A young girl answered and smiled welcoming to first Father Mac and then more closely at Beth. "Aunt Lucy is this way," she motioned for them to proceed her. In the middle of the living room stood a large boned, rather elegant lady with silver gray hair and a pair of the bluest, sharpest eyes Beth had ever seen. They also held a twinkle as both looked each other over.

Beth recovered first and asked rather impishly "Well, do I pass inspection, Miss Donovan?"

"Humph. Young ladies should be seen and not heard. I might know that Murphy would never get himself hooked up with some proper, shy young thing," Miss Lucy retorted.

"Miss Lucy," Beth interrupted, "were you ever a shy, proper young thing?"

Blue eyes looked even closer at Beth, "No, I wasn't. And if I were fifty years younger, I'd have given you a run for your money with young Murphy. Now there is a man. Not sops like some of them. Looks like he picked himself a girl with sass. Finally showing some good sense." She turned to Father Mac, "Well, don't just stand there, we don't wait on formality here. Sit down."

Father Mac nodded, sat and continued to shake his head at the two women in the room. Beth sat opposite Miss Lucy and her eyes took a quick appraisal of the room. "Very nice," she thought, liking the colonial pieces of furniture. Turning her head, she stared. There in the corner was a piano, a console, not very elaborate. Beth swallowed and without even realizing it rose and walked over to the bench. She ran her hand experimentally over the keys. The sound hit a distant chord in her memory. As a person who is starved of water for a long period would drink thirstily, so Beth took great pleasure in the feel of the keys. She sat down. Forgetting Father Mac and Miss Lucy, Beth began to play and as she played, she sang. A sound soft as the birds in the morning, as gentle as the rain came pouring forth from her. Song after song came forth. When she had finished, she looked up, almost surprised to see Father and Miss Lucy in the same room. A blush rose in her cheeks, "I'm so sorry ...please forgive me," Beth mumbled to Miss Lucy.

"Can you play 'Danny Boy,' child?" The imperious voice asked softly. A nod and Beth looked down at the keys again, her voice clear and true this time with a soft Irish lilt to the words. On the last note, Beth looked up. Tears flowed down her face. There were tears on Miss Lucy's cheeks as glistening eyes shone on Beth.

"Father Mac," Miss Lucy whispered, "the Whitaker's may purchase anything they wish, but the piano... "she paused, "is my wedding gift to them." At Beth's surprised look, and instant murmuring of refusal, she held up her hand. "Please Beth, to make an old woman happy. To hear you sing that song as I heard it in my youth was like an angel calling to my very soul. For me to know that someone such as yourself had my things, I would know they would be taken care of. A washer, a dryer can be fixed, repaired, replaced, but a piano has feelings and to involve those feelings as you just did is a gift very few possess." She paused, sniffed into her handkerchief. "Just give me the pieces you wish to purchase; I'll feel good about them going to someone like you and Murphy. Just promise me that you'll be happy with Murphy..."

"I will do my best to make Murphy happy," Beth answered solemnly. Still Father Mac sat, as if turned to stone. He stared at the young girl seated before him.

He cleared his throat. "Miss Lucy, if you would be so kind as to sit through one more song. Beth, can you sing 'Ave Maria'?"

Beth began again, this time her voice raising, falling, each note clear. A chill went up their spine as those listening recognized the gift of the young girl whose voice had touched their hearts. Much later in the car, Beth broke the silence. "Father Mac, I'm sorry for upsetting you."

"Oh, child," Father replied, "I'm not upset. Stunned is the word. To hear a voice such as yours here ...how, why?"

Beth felt drained, "It's a long story, Father ... "She told her story briefly. She finished as she pulled into the lane. "Please, Father, don't say anything about my singing, I still don't feel comfortable about things."

Father Mac nodded, "As you wish, Beth, and ...thank you." Beth looked up astonished, "...for the rare opportunity of hearing a nightingale," he finished.

The next two weeks followed in a whirlwind of activity. Each day brought more people to help. Each day they went home tired but completely won over by the new mistress of the Whitaker farm. Each evening after they had gone, Beth worked late into the night sewing on curtains, drapes, bedspreads. She and Casey, who was up and around now, also worked on a few toys for the children. Casey was refinishing a wooden horse, a small wagon and a dollhouse they found in the attic. During the days, Casey whittled furniture and toy soldiers and tiny animal figurines. Beth made Raggedy Ann and Andy dolls, clothes from the drapery scraps and tiny curtains and spreads for the dollhouse as well. Casey and Beth were the odd couple at best, but Casey was devoted to the young lass and she was very protective of her friend. The workroom off the garage had been remodeled to form a room for Casey and

Bingo, he claimed it not proper for him to sleep in the house with her unchaperoned. Anyone seeing the house would hardly recognize the same beautiful well-kept yards and field, the freshly painted fences and buildings to the same derelict shadows of only a few days.

Such was how Murphy saw it as he turned his truck into the lane late one evening, two weeks later.

CHAPTER 6

Murphy was tired. It had been a hectic two weeks, finding good livestock, getting all the paperwork settled, arranging for feed and transportation. It'll be good to be home," he thought. Home, strange how it had been a long time since he had felt he had a home, rooms, but not a home. His thoughts roamed to hazel eyes, an elfin face and a dimple that couldn't be hidden, I wonder how she is, how much she got done. Poor thing, I never should have left her there alone. Well things didn't cost quite as much as I thought, they had a few good bargains in cattle. Maybe we can swing a few workmen into spruce things up. Lord knows I certainly won't have time...the fields to plow, and plant...getting the livestock set up. Murphy was excited, a deep exhilaration filling his mind. It felt good to be getting back to the soil. Over the years he had often wished he had never left the farm.

Murphy shook his head, as much to clear the cobwebs as to keep himself awake. He turned the truck into the lane and stopped, slamming on the brakes. He slid to a stop only inches away from the freshly painted fence. Murphy stared at the panorama spread out before him. It was as if he stepped back into time when his grandfather still lived. The lane was lined with a white wooden fence, beyond the fence were rolling fields, already plowed and tilled, ready for planting.

Murphy set his chin and restarted the truck. He drove slowly down the lane taking in the freshly painted buildings. Then he saw the house. No longer a rundown heirloom, but a glistening colonial treasure. Flowers peeped from the window boxes, roses had been trimmed and already had begun climbing the trellis guarding the gate.

A strange dog barked a warning, as an angry Murphy stepped out of the truck. Long quick strides carried him to the back door and into the kitchen filled with the sweet smell of the fresh baked pies and a roast simmering gently in the oven. A quick glance barely took in the fresh paint or wallpaper. "Beth," Murphy called harshly. "Beth!" Came the sharp command. As he heard no answer, Murphy crossed the kitchen and headed for the stairs.

"Beth!" he called again, his steps taking them two at a time. At the top of the stairs he paused. He heard the laughter of Beth and ...My God she's with a man, in my home! With the quiet tread of a lion about to pounce Murphy crossed the hall to stand outside the bedroom door.

"Perfect," he heard Beth say, "I love ..."

Murphy threw the door open, anger emanating from his body. Cold dark eyes searched the room for Beth. I'll kill him, Murphy thought, when his eyes found them. Murphy stopped dead in his tracks, for there atop a ladder sat Beth, putting on the finishing touches to the drapes she was hanging. At the bottom of the ladder stood a dark figure, Murphy's hands tightened into fists, as he took two steps toward the man. He turned, Murphy stopped, astonishment filled his face as he recognized the clerical collar.

63

"... the effect, don't you?" Beth finished. When she turned to Father Mac, she saw Murphy. "Murphy! Oh no! I wanted to have it all done and be outside waiting for you. I just couldn't imagine your face. What do you think?" She rushed on seemingly oblivious to the tension between Murphy and Father Mac. "Oh, I am sorry," she went on, "Murphy this is Father John MacNair, pastor of St. Mary's. Father Mac this is my husband, Murphy."

The two men looked at each other, measuring up the worth of their opponent. MacNair wondered if this anger was always there, and if so, he wanted to protect this young girl. Murphy saw a priest, but a man, nonetheless. Slowly Murphy raised his hand, "Hello Father." He stated coolly, still assessing the man before him.

"Hello, my son," MacNair said, and firmly clasped his hand, for he had seen the jealousy in the young man's eyes and realized his thoughts. He's young, thought MacNair, how anyone could think of young Beth in that way, but love isn't always clear.

Beth started down the ladder, only to be clasped firmly halfway down by two strong arms and deposited safely to the floor. The nearness of Murphy made Beth feel warm. His hands lingered on her waist. Beth looked up, her face only inches from Murphy's. For a few seconds Beth stared at the firm lips as they came down to meet hers. It was as if an electric shock coursed through her as his lips met hers. A slow melting of her legs left Beth feeling strangely bereft as Murphy raised his head. His voice strangely hoarse as he whispered. "It's good to be home, wife."

Beth still stunned by her reaction to his kiss slowly realized it was only for Father Mac's benefit. She grinned shakily, "Welcome home, husband!" Turning slowly in his arms, Beth spoke to both men. "How about some coffee and pie? Father Mac? Murphy?... "

Murphy nodded, and Father Mac grinned sheepishly. "I think I'll take a raincheck, Beth. I somehow feel it's time you two newlyweds were alone without me. I don't think you need a chaperone!"

Beth didn't stop him as Murphy's hands dug into her waist as if to signal her. "Thanks, Father, for all your help and of St. Mary's," Beth replied.

"No child, no thanks were needed. I'll see you both at Mass. Good night Murphy, I'll see myself out." With that he left, leaving Beth still standing in Murphy's arms.

Beth stood still, she heard the front door close, then she gently pulled free of Murphy's arms. She felt suddenly shy.

"How?" Murphy's harsh voice broke the stillness.

"I thought you'd be pleased," Beth murmured, shocked at the anger she saw in his flashing eyes.

"Pleased? Pleased? Just how did you think I'd be pleased at the stack of bills you've hidden away for all this work? You knew we could only spend the farm's money. You knew the conditions of the will. Why couldn't you do the work yourself? No patience? Or just not used to physical, manual labor. Pleased? I feel like wringing your neck!" Murphy spoke each word deliberately, his face darkened by the anger he was holding leased inside.

"Murphy," Beth began, her voice trembling, "if you'll just listen, I can explain everything. It's all right, all the bills have been paid ... "

As he grabbed her arm, Murphy sneered, "And how did they get paid, Beth, did you mortgage the farm or sell your favors to everyone in town including our friendly priest!"

Without thinking, Beth's free hand came up and slapped the sneer on his face. No longer trembling with fear but anger, Beth lashed out as well, "How dare you? ... How dare you judge everyone by your own crude behavior or by the seemingly tasteless women you've always surrounded yourself with. Don't touch me, I don't even want to stay in the same room with you." She pulled away from Murphy and walked to the door, "You can talk to me when you're willing to listen to reason, but remember one thing, Mr. Whitaker, I have done nothing...nothing wrong to you...to the will, to anybody!" On the last word she slammed the door shut, ran down the hall, and out the front door. She drew in great gasps of fresh air hoping to cool her temper and calm her tattered nerves. How dare he say that. Think that! Didn't he even know the kind of women she was? No, her conscience spoke back, he doesn't. Let's be reasonable, he doesn't know you at all. He leaves for two weeks and comes home to a different picture without any inkling of how or what it took to get it done and Father Mac was there. Oh Murphy... Beth sighed; how can I explain if you won't even listen to me. She buried her face in her arms by the fence, lost in thoughts and plans of how to best explain things to Murphy.

From the bedroom window, Murphy had not moved. He had let Beth walk out, let her runaway, more to keep himself from hurting her than anything else. A deep breath seemed to come from Murphy's very soul as he watched her figure cross the yard and lean against the fence. His anger was leaving him slowly as he too tried to justify his outburst and accusations to himself. You're not fair, you don't know her, deep inside he knew that Beth was not like the other women he had known. There was a softness about her mouth ...She had seemed to melt in his arms, so sweet. But that was always one of their ploys, his mind fought back ...Give her a chance to explain, it can't be any worse than what your mind is thinking. Just listen, she had said, for just a second Murphy's harshness disappeared, she is a spunky little thing. He touched his jaw; she also packs a pretty good wallop for a girl. Murphy turned and headed for the door, not seeing as he turned that Beth had left her stand and had started walking toward the house.

They met at the front door, both surprised to find the other. Beth set a nervous tongue over suddenly dry lips. "Murphy, if you'll just set down and listen, I can explain...Please," she looked at the impassive face of Murphy.

He wasn't giving anything away, but he nodded "I'll listen."

Beth gave a sigh of relief, "How ... How about in the kitchen over a cup of coffee and...a piece of pie?" Her voice had dwindled to almost a whisper, her courage suddenly disappearing.

A slight twitch hit the corner of his mouth, almost as if he was suppressing a smile. He looked down at Beth and said dryly, "The way to a man's heart is through his stomach, right?"

Beth gave a weak grin in return, "Not really, I just felt with a fork in one hand and a coffee cup in the other, I might have a fighting chance."

Murphy shook his head. "No chance, wife, head in."

In the kitchen, Beth was very aware of Murphy's presence. He sat at the table and watched as she got two cups, filled them and cut the pie. As she turned to set them on the table, she met his glance and said, "A condemned man eats a hearty breakfast...er...snack in this case." Murphy gave a wry grin, "start talking." He took a bite of pie and turned surprised eyes to Beth.

Beth grinned showing the dimple, "In answer to your question, yes, I made it and no, it isn't poisoned! You needn't look so surprised; I have a few talents hidden away."

"It's very good. I guess this means I won't starve in the future?" He raised questioning eyebrows at Beth.

"Well that depends," She retorted, "well here goes... remember now, just listen. When you left, I worked around the house but then I took a sandwich and went for a walk, more to get a breather than anything else. In the orchard, I ran into Father Mac. Over the past five years the parish has been tending the fruit trees for your grandfather. Matt paid them per hour and then a percentage of the ripened fruit. Well, they continued even after they passed away. Father Mac gave me a check and an account stub of the last two years. It was for almost $20,000."

She saw the look of shock on his face. "I mentioned it to you when you called, you seemed to think it a little amount and you said to spend it on the house. I tried to tell you how much it was, but you hung up. The more I thought it seemed the ideal solution. You said we had enough to get started but the improvements had to be held off for a while. I didn't know what arrangements you were going to do in the orchard, so I hired the church to help me clean and paint and everything. Most of the furniture is what your grandparents had, but some I bought second hand from Miss Lucy Donavan, she knew you, she gave us the piano as a wedding present. I made the curtains and bedspreads and Casey, and I are fixing the toys." Beth ended in a rush, she looked up to find Murphy's quizzical eyes on her. They held surprise and a touch of something Beth didn't understand.

Murphy was quiet, he finally asked, "Casey?"

"Oh, yes," Beth again swept her tongue over her lips. "well," she began, "he's the same man who helped your grandparents, years ago. He was living in a tiny shack over by the orchard. I found him sick." Beth paused. "Don't be mad, Murphy, but I've hired him back and he's living in a small room in the garage." She looked up at him, long lashes brushing over eyes wide and a little apprehensive as to Murphy's acceptance of Casey.

"How much is left of the money, Beth?" Murphy's voice was low and held no trace of anger.

"Almost half," Beth answered.

"Then that's more than enough to help us pay Casey this year if we include his board and keep," he added.

Relief swept over Beth, "Oh, Murphy, thank you, thank you!" Without thinking she jumped up and kissed Murphy's rather astonished cheek. "Now," Beth bubbled on, "let me give you a grand tour before supper." Grabbing his hand, she led Murphy throughout the house. Showing him the pantry, the utility room complete with washer and dryer and freezer. The living room and dining room already had flowers in them, everything was sparkling clean and showed the old pieces of furniture, not as old, but comfortable. The house was a home with character. The den was masculine and ready for occupancy. Murphy walked through the house, making no comment, but his eyes missed nothing. When they got to the children's bedrooms, Beth stopped. She looked apprehensively at the tall, giant of a man beside her. "Murphy, please say something. If you don't like it, I'll repaint, whatever. Tell me you hate it but say something ... "her eyes looked pleadingly at his face willing him to speak.

Murphy looked at the upturned face. He placed his hands on either side of her face, he bent down and gently kissed Beth. "Thank you," he whispered. "If I could have hired someone, told them my ideas, this is what it would have looked like. You turned the house into a very warm country home. It shows gracious lines and perfect taste while still being practical and very livable. You are a strange girl, Beth. Your Uncle Henry was right." His voice was firm, but his sincerity was unmistakable.

His words of praise filled Beth's heart; her face glowed as did her eyes. A smile lit her features as the dimple in her cheek appeared. "Oh, Murphy. I am so glad. Now, how was your trip? Did you get all the livestock? What kind will we have? Can we have some kittens and a puppy...for the kids you know," she laughed "well, actually for me, but I promise to share with them."

Murphy laughed too. "Yes, to everything! Anything special in mind?"

"Well," she said wryly, "as a matter of fact, Joe Mortland has the cutest little puppies and Miss Lucy has these 2 cats, Hansel and Gretel. She can't take them with her and as Gretel's in the family way, I was hoping we might take care of them. We need a few mouse traps anyway, right"

Murphy nodded and grinned, "Unless I'm mistaken, this is a con job. Let me see, you've already said yes and probably have already made arrangements as to when we get them." He looked at Beth shrewdly, "hum?"

"Would I do anything like that?" Beth asked innocently.

As if on cue, Casey's voice was heard from the kitchen door. "Miss Beth...Miss Beth, I finished the doghouse. Do you want to see it before I paint the name on?"

Murphy threw back his head and laughed, a deep rumble. Beth joined in and together they went to find Casey. Murphy and Beth entered the kitchen still chuckling, his arm rested lightly on her shoulder. To Casey, they looked like a young couple very much in love and very happy. He joined in their smiles and reached out to clasp the hand of the young man by Beth's side. "Evening, Mr. Murphy. Sure, am glad to have you come back."

"It's nice to be back, Casey, especially knowing you're still here to help out. I'll rest a lot easier with your knowledge to fall back on. Thanks for coming back to help us."

Murphy's words erased the doubts Casey had that he might not be welcome. He swept his hands over his eyes and looked back at Murphy and Beth. Beth was touched that Murphy had made such an effort to make Casey feel welcome and needed. She reached for his hand and squeezed it.

"How about some supper?" Beth queried, "Now you two get cleaned up while I set the table and dish the food out. Now scoot, I'm serving in five minutes. If you're not here, you'll tryout that doghouse before Joe's dog!"

"Let's go, Casey, she sounds like she means business. Tell me, does her cooking taste as good as it smells?"

They walked out together to wash up. Beth shook her head. "What a combination," she thought. But we'll make it. She was feeling very proud of her husband. Today she felt she had pierced his barriers. She had seen warmth, gentleness and concern for someone else. He'll be all right if I just get him to show that he cares and not keep it all locked away. She hummed as she set out dinner.

Dinner was a light-hearted meal. Both men tried to outdo the other in complimenting the cook. Beth took their praise in stride, then switched the topic to crops and the livestock Murphy had bought.

"Most of it should arrive tomorrow and Friday," he told Casey. "I've got Herefords coming tomorrow along with some New Hampshire's. Friday we should have Yorkshire pork coming by truck. With the fields ready, we can start planting right away." He noticed Beth's blank look of comprehension over the information and smiled, "You do know what a Hereford is?"

"Well, no...not exactly," Beth said, disarmed by the warmth of his smile. "I assume it's some kind of farm animal."

Murphy and Casey laughed, "Right, let's start you out on being a farmer's wife." Murphy began, "Cattle, hogs and poultry are the chief sources of farm income in this country. Herefords are a type of cattle that have red bodies and white faces. They can be grazed on grasslands or corn fed. If corn fed their meat is tastier. That's what we'll be doing. Yorkshires are a breed of hogs. They're white and have erect ears. It's a leading bacon producing variety which grows swiftly, produces large litters and yields a lot of meat not fat. Chickens can be raised for their egg laying ability or for the meat. New Hampshire's supply both. They're reddish in color and not as prone to disease as other varieties." He grinned, "Does that help you at all?"

Beth returned the grin, "Sure does, we're getting cows and chickens tomorrow and pigs on Friday."

"In a nutshell, yes," Murphy laughed.

"What, if anything, needs to be done to get ready for the animals?" he queried to Casey.

Casey nodded knowingly, "Luke Brown has hay he can sell us pretty reasonably. We'll need feed for the hogs and chickens. The grain elevator in Alton might have it the cheapest but it might not be of consistent quality. The Seed & Feed in Hardin is a little higher, but it might be better in the long run."

Murphy leaned back in his chair, "Let's call Luke tonight and set up delivery tomorrow. We'll also go with the Seed & Feed. Can you call first thing in the morning, Casey, and order ...let's see, we'll need a good supply of corn, sorghum, barley, wheat, rye and oats for the hogs. A meal of fish, bone and milk for the chickens, and corn, hay and sorghum for the cows. Also salt blocks for the animals." He scratched some figures on a scrap of paper for Casey. "That's enough to get us started and to be delivered tomorrow by noon if possible. Go ahead then and fix up a bi-weekly delivery system."

"Will do, sir, first thing." Casey pushed back his chair.

Beth reached out to stop him. She touched his arm. "Casey, what about the toys? Won't you be helping me anymore?"

"Oh, I'll still be helping you, Miss Beth, but I'll do it in my room. Mr. Murphy will be here to help you." Casey's voice was firm. He was not going to be in the way of these two.

"Casey," Murphy interrupted, "I think Beth is asking, will you please stay the evening and help us finish up the toys. You see, she's not quite sure yet whether I'll be a help or hindrance."

Casey smiled, "Well, if you're sure, I'll just go collect the pieces." He turned at the door, pulled himself up to his full five foot plus and looked Murphy in the eye and said, "I...I'll just say this once sir, I appreciate you're taking me on, and I'll see you won't be sorry. Not you or Miss Beth. Just thank her." He left, a slight little man but with his pride intact.

Beth got up and started to clear the table, surprised when Murphy began washing the dishes. Companionably they washed, dried and put them away. Together they helped carry the toys out. Beth finished putting the curtains up in the doll house, Casey continued whittling the little animals, and Murphy began painting the horse and wagon. Casey broke the easy silence by asking if Miss Beth was going to sing tonight. Beth shook her head, suddenly shy to sing before Murphy.

"Please, Beth," Murphy said softly. Beth looked at the eyes resting on her, the twinkling blue of Casey's and the soft dark blue of Murphy's. She started humming the old ballads Casey liked so well, drifting into song. Her voice rose and fell. Murphy stopped working and stared at Beth. Her voice was beautiful, he thought, almost as beautiful as he was learning Beth was. His thoughts were interrupted by the ringing of the telephone. Beth stopped and walked to the phone.

"Saved by the bell," she quipped. "Hello," she spoke into the receiver.

"Is this Murphy Whitaker's home?" a harsh voice asked.

"Yes, it is," Beth answered, "Who is calling?"

"You must be Murphy's new bride, just get him. Tell him it's his darling sister-in-law." The voice waited.

Beth looked at the phone. She swallowed, "Murphy," she said, "It's for you. I think it's Celia." She raised a worried, suddenly solemn face to Murphy as he took the phone. She started to return to her seat, but Murphy reached out and caught her arm. "This concerns you, too," he said.

Beth gave him a thumbs up signal, "Good luck," she whispered.

Murphy suddenly bent down and brushed her lips with a hard, brief kiss. "That's for luck," he said to her surprised look. He took the phone in one hand and rested his arm around Beth's shoulders. "Hello, Celia," he said, "what gives us the pleasure of your call?"

"Murphy, darling, you took your sweet time. Did I interrupt anything important between your new wife and her loving husband?" A deep throaty laugh followed.

"Nothing we can't continue later," Murphy replied. Beth blushed overhearing the remark on the phone. "What is it, Celia?"

"My, my, you are the impatient lover, aren't you?" she drawled. "I'll be quick, just for you dear. I'm bringing the kids tomorrow around 5:00. If I can find your farm, oh and by the way, I'm also bringing my lawyer along to take pictures so we can show the hovel you want to keep Joanna's children in, the judge should find it interesting, don't you think?"

"I'm sure he will. We'll see you tomorrow night. Just a minute, what is it Beth?"

She looked up from Murphy's arm, "Do they want to stay and have supper with us?"

"Celia? Beth wants to know if you'd like to stay and eat with us? Who knows, you can take pictures and show the judge how we feed the children too," he said smoothly, sarcasm underlying his tone.

"Lovely, we'll be there. See you then." The line went dead. Murphy turned to Beth, "Tomorrow at 5:00 and yes, they'll be here for supper."

"Did she mention how the children were, Murphy?" Beth queried.

"Not a word, only threats from her about the pictures her lawyer is going to take of the farm," he said darkly. He grinned suddenly. "Thanks to you and St. Mary's is she in for a surprise!"

Beth returned his smile. She turned to Casey, "Do you think we can finish up tonight? Jenny and Mike are coming, and I want everything to be waiting for them, all ready. It might make them feel a little more at home."

"We'll do it, Miss," Casey assured her. "We'll have her finished in another hour at most." He bent to his task with renewed vigilance. Beth and Murphy followed suit. As each was finished, they carried them up and put them in the bedrooms, the wagon, horse and soldiers for Mike, the dolls and dollhouse for Jenny.

Casey left, whistling as he walked, Bingo close at his heels. Beth and Murphy watched him go, quiet, each in their own thoughts of tomorrow. "Bedtime," Murphy drawled, "off you go. You can have the bathroom first. I'll lock up and be up in a little while, okay?"

Beth nodded nervously. Aware suddenly that she was going to sleep in the same room as this man, what if...what if, Beth swallowed. "Murphy... " it came out in little more than a croak.

"Beth," Murphy stopped her. "Today I started believing in someone, started to trust when I haven't trusted anyone in years. I'm not going to do anything to break that fragile thread. I find I quite like my new wife, my friend. Can you begin to like me, just a little, too?"

Beth reached up, kissed his cheek and walked to the doorway. There she turned, "Sleep tight, friend," she whispered and went upstairs to bed feeling very safe.

CHAPTER 7

Beth woke to the sound of the shower running. Better hurry, she thought and jumped up to gather the clothes she would wear that day. She had just put on her robe when a knock on the door warned her of Murphy's entrance into the room.

"It's all yours," he said as he crossed the room to the small dressing room off the bedroom. Beth was struck afresh by his broad shoulders, his powerful legs.

"Murphy," she said, "won't Celia think it odd that you knock before you enter your own room?"

"Probably," he said, "but I just couldn't come barging in without giving you any notice. I wouldn't mind your state of undress, but I think you might!"

"I do appreciate it. I just want things to look as normal as possible for Celia and everyone else," Beth went on to explain. "Maybe if you just wake me before you go to take a shower, I'll be ready when you return?"

Murphy nodded in agreement. "That should do it." He walked into the dressing room and began whistling. He stuck his head around the door for a minute, "Hey, wife, what does a man have to do to get breakfast around here?"

Beth made a face at him, "Give me twenty minutes and it'll be on the table...IF...you're a good husband and leave me to get moving!" Beth hummed as she took a quick shower, dressed in jeans and a print cotton blouse.

She tied back her hair with a ribbon, slipped sandals on and hurried down the stairs.

In the kitchen, she started coffee and put the bacon on. Taking out flour, milk and eggs, she started mixing pancakes. What a beautiful morning, Beth thought. She hummed as she flipped the golden pancakes and turned crisp bacon. Setting the table was accomplished just as Murphy came down the stairs.

"Something sure smells good!" He told her smiling.

Beth smiled, "It's nice to be appreciated. I did want to talk to you for just a minute if I could, though."

"Complaints already?" he asked.

"No, but I'll let you know when I do," she retorted. "It's about food. I can cook plain simple fare but nothing fancy. Are these meals alright with you or should I take a Cordon Bleu course?"

"These are fine. Better than that! I never really was one for fancy meals anyhow. Isn't that what you go out to restaurants for?"

"Good," Beth sighed. "Now, about the freezer. Is it okay if I stock up at the meat locker in Elsah or do you plan on butchering in the next couple of days? Also, about the kittens and puppy?" she hesitated. "They will be here tonight," she added.

"Right," Murphy said. "Fill the freezer at the locker, meat, vegetables, whatever. Casey and I will be busy with livestock today, so if you take the wagon, we'll help you unload when you get home. Stop by and see Joe and Lucy and bring the entire crew home with you." He paused, "Anything else?" She shook her head. "Good. Lunch about 1:00. Something light in the fridge and Casey and I will take care of ourselves. I know you've got a busy day planned. Keep supper simple and, Beth," he warned, "relax, stop worrying. You'll be fine with the kids. Celia," he said ominously, "doesn't count." with that, he and Casey left, with a hasty, "Thankee ma'am," from Casey. Cleaning up the kitchen and stacking the dishes, Beth cut up roast beef leftovers for sandwiches and made a salad as well, placing both in the refrigerator as Murphy had instructed.

She ran the sweeper, dusted, cleaned the bathroom and put fresh sheets on the children's' beds. Taking the wet towels and dirty clothes downstairs, she threw a load in the washer and sat down to make up a list of food for the freezer and pantry.

"Baked chicken," she thought, "for tonight's meal. That's simple and almost everybody likes chicken, mashed potatoes, gravy, peas, fresh baked rolls and a special dessert. We'll just see what the locker has."

She grabbed her purse and headed for the car, waving at Casey and Murphy as she started the car. Both men were engrossed in unloading the hay Luke had just pulled in with.

Beth sang softly as she drove the short distance to the store and locker. She bought mounds of food it seemed, roasts, steaks, hamburger, chicken, fish, lots of frozen vegetables and even some frozen fruit. "Strawberry shortcake! That will be for tonight. Perfect, let's hope I can get it all done." She had them load it in the car, then made a quick trip to Joe's to get her puppy, a soft brown and white bundle of fur. He joyfully licked her face as she headed to Miss Lucy's to pick up Hansel and Gretel.

She found that was her first error. Do not mix cats and dogs in a car with groceries! Thank heavens it was a short trip home as the puppy whimpered in her lap and the cats hissed from the other side of the car.

Beth honked as she pulled into the yard and sure enough Murphy came out of the house to help her unload. His dust streaked face creased into a smile as he watched Beth try to keep the puppy and the two cats from each other while still holding onto her purse. Ruefully Beth turned the snarling cats over to him, as she shifted the weight of the puppy. Both purred contentedly as Murphy put them on the ground by the porch and fed them some milk. Beth hooked the puppy to his doghouse to keep him from running underfoot while they unloaded the car. They were only halfway done when two trucks pulled into the lane.

Beth spoke from behind Murphy, "Go on, I'll manage."

He turned and she almost collided with him as Hansel weaved herself in and out of their legs. He caught her in his strong clasp, "Easy does it. I'll bring in the boxes of meat. You unload, okay?" he grinned. "Anyway, it'll take them a while to fix up the ramps to unload the animals."

Even after he had removed his hands Beth could still feel the warmth of his grasp. Careful, girl she cautioned herself. Friends only, remember? She hurried back into the kitchen to put things away and begin the preparations for dinner. At 4:00 things were moving smoothly, dinner was progressing, the clothes were put away, the puppy and cats settled nicely. Beth decided to take a quick shower and change.

Running upstairs, she showered, shampooed her hair, crossed the hall and donned first underwear, she blew her hair dry, glad to see it fall in soft waves about her face. A touch of eyeshadow, mascara, blusher and lipstick, she slipped a pale green dress over her head, its soft material clinging to her slim body. As she hunted for her sandals, Murphy walked into the room. He stopped as he saw her. "Sorry, Beth. I thought you were still in the shower."

"No harm done," Beth assured him. "This time it's all yours." She bent her head to fasten her sandals on. She missed the appreciative gleam in his eyes as they moved lingeringly over the soft curves of her breast, the tiny span of her waist and the promise of her tender lips.

"Better hurry," she said as she passed him at the door and walked swiftly down to put the finishing touches to their dinner.

She heard Murphy come down the stairs and gave him a wolf whistle as he rounded the door. A grin replaced the stern set of his chin. Almost involuntarily his hand went to touch his scar. Beth tried to ease his fears. "Yes, even with your scar. It makes you different. You're not just another pretty face."

With that Murphy started laughing. "Well, that's certainly good to hear!" He was still laughing when the knock came at the door. Beth gave him a thumbs up sign as he walked to open it. She held her breath.

As Murphy opened the door, his smile froze as," Oh! my God, your face!" was heard from Celia, Beth assumed. Walking forward, she put her arm around Murphy's waist, "Come in," she said. She felt the tenseness in Murphy and knew the lines of his face were again set in grim lines. She looked at him hoping to catch his glance, but he remained unyielding.

Beth looked at her guests. First to the voice she recognized as Celia's. A tall, blonde sophisticate stared critically back at her. Beside her stood a man of medium height, nondescript really, Beth thought, compared to my Murphy. Her gaze followed downwards to two pairs of solemn blue eyes. Both had the same dark hair as Murphy. Jenny's long and tied with a ribbon. Mike's cut barely keeping it from his eyes. Round faces with slight bodies, they were beautiful. Jenny was dressed in ruffles from head to foot in a pale pink dress. Mike had a light blue suit on complete with tie.

Beth smiled and put out her hand, "Hello, Jenny...Mike. We are very glad you've come." She shook the tiny hand of Jenny and the larger one of Mike.

A muffled "How do you do." came from Mike.

Beth looked at Murphy, her eyes imploring him to speak to the children. He saw her look, gave her hand a gentle squeeze and put out his hand to Mike. "Hello, Mike, Jenny. Beth has already told you how happy we are to have you here. We've done a lot to get things ready for you. Would you like to see your rooms?" He turned to Beth, "Can supper wait just a little while?"

Beth's smile was radiant. "Of course." She squeezed his hand as she reached for Jenny and Mike's. "Come this way, please."

They formed a strange procession going up the stairs. Murphy leading, Beth between the two small children and Celia and her friend, not to be left behind, following closely in their wake. Celia's face was set. The beautiful home was not what she had expected, and she had not been prepared for the young girl who had such an effect on Murphy.

Murphy led them to Jenny's room first. He turned the lights on and watched her face as she looked from the dollhouse to the wide selection of doll clothes for the Raggedy Ann and Andy dolls. She slowly walked over to the dresser and picked up the tiny wooden animals on the dresser. A solitary tear trickled down her cheek as she turned to face Beth and Murphy. She walked over to Beth and kissed her cheek. Beth gave her a hug in return. Then she turned to Murphy, "Oh, please," Beth prayed, "please let Murphy see he doesn't frighten you." She burst out crying as she flung herself into his arms, holding onto his neck for dear life.

"It's all right," he whispered into her hair, "go ahead and cry, baby, it's all right ..."

Tears fell down Beth's cheeks before she was even aware of them. "Thank you, oh thank God," she whispered. She squeezed Mike's hand. "Would you like to see your room now? Come this way. Uncle Murphy and Jenny can join us in a little while."

At Mike's nod, she led him across the hall. She watched as his face lit up at the horse. When he walked over to the wagon, he gave a small shout. "Oh neato!" He found the toy soldiers Casey had whittled, "These are terrific. Thank you," he said and smiled warmly up at Beth.

Beth smiled at him in return. "You're very welcome, although I didn't do the soldiers. At dinner tonight I'll introduce you to Casey. He whittles those and the tiny animals in Jenny's room out of wood. If you ask him, he'll show you how he does it and maybe make something else for you."

A wistful note crept into Mike's voice as he spoke, "I would like that. Maybe I can ask him to make a kitten for Jenny. She won't ask him herself."

"She's just shy," Beth tried to reassure him. "She's been through a lot. Just give her time."

Celia spoke up, her presence forgotten by Beth. "She'll need more than time. She hasn't spoken since we told them her parents were dead." She turned on her heel and walked out of the room.

Beth smiled at the solemn Mike, shaken by the words, yet seeking to reassure the young boy at her side. "We'll help her, Mike. The death of your parents left a scar on Jenny's mind. She doesn't want to talk, but scars heal. Look at your Uncle Murphy. He had an accident which hurt him terribly. It left a scar, but the scar is only a remembrance now of what happened. Jenny's scars will heal, too, and soon they'll be only memories. That's when she'll talk. Until then, she's got you and me and Uncle Murphy to help her. Now," she straightened up, "I think we'd better eat before it burns up. Let's go see if Jenny is ready to join us."

Together they walked to her door. She still lay in Murphy's arms. Her sobs had ended and just an occasional hiccup could be heard.

"Anyone in here hungry?" Beth asked quietly.

"We sure are," Murphy answered. "Aren't we Jenny? After supper Beth has another surprise to show to you, so let's go eat. Mike, do you and Jenny want to wash up before we eat?"

As they left the room, his questioning prompted Beth to tell him about Jenny. Then she looked up at Murphy, "You were super with Jenny. She'll be okay, just give her time." She held his gaze for several seconds. She felt very close to Murphy. His eyes were warm, inviting. Beth's bones seemed to melt as he slowly leaned forward.

The moment was broken by Celia's cry, "Are we ever going to eat?"

"Go on," Murphy said ruefully, "I'll bring the kids while you serve up. Better hurry, it sounds as if she's going to have Casey as an appetizer."

Beth hurried down the stairs and to the kitchen. There she found a rather subdued Casey, sitting calmly at the kitchen table.

"Miss Beth," he began, "if it's all the same to you I think I'll eat in the kitchen tonight."

Beth sat down and took Casey's hand, "NO Casey, it isn't. You see, Mike and Jenny are here. They loved the animals and wooden soldiers more than anything else. I promised to introduce you to them. Besides, you're family...and I ... I need all the support I can muster to get through tonight." She looked at Casey and smiled a grin that brought out the dimple. "I never thought leprechauns were afraid of anything!"

Casey smiled back, "For you, Miss Beth. I'm only doing this for you. But saints preserve us if that woman stays for any length of time!"

Murphy put his head around the door, "Need any help?"

"Everything is under control. Do you want to seat them? Casey and I will be right in," Beth spoke cheerfully, "Won't we, Casey?"

Casey only mumbled, took the platter and disappeared past an astonished Murphy.

Dinner progressed smoothly, despite Celia's monologue of the tedious flight, the children's activities and her own achievements. Beth was very quiet, feeling it wiser to listen. Celia however read her quietness as something quite different.

"Murphy, how clever of you," Celia crooned.

He looked up, "In what way?" he asked politely.

"Why to get such a wife. While she's not bad to look at, she's such a timid little mouse. Definitely wise, she's so different from Joanna, isn't she?"

Beth looked up, surprise on her face. Celia purred, knowing by the look on Beth's face she was in ignorance of her next words, "Oh, but surely you've told your wife all about your last fiancé and how she left you for your own brother, haven't you Murphy dear?"

Beth's eyes flew to him, but Murphy wasn't talking, his face was taunt, his scar stood out. "It didn't concern us or our future, Celia." He said, tongue in cheek. "I shall have to remind you, we have other guests present," he motioned to the children sitting wide-eyed, not understanding the words but sensing the tension.

Beth put down her fork, she smiled at the children," Are you ready for that surprise, now? Casey will you come with us to help me?"

Casey threw her a grateful glance, "Yes, Ma'am...Come on young feller," he directed at Mike, "and you little lady." Beth let her eyes set for just a moment on her husband, almost asking for some sign that Celia's malicious remarks weren't true. Murphy sat, staring down at his plate, his face like granite, his eyes as they reached Beth's cold. For a second, Beth thought he was about to say something but changed his mind.

"Murphy," Beth asked, unaware of the pleading uncertainness in her voice, "would you like to come along, too?"

87

"I'd like a breath of fresh air, yes," He said barely keeping his anger under control. He turned to Celia and her friend, "In the future, don't you ever say anything else in front of those children about their mother and me, they can hear, and they'll remember. You will not spoil any memories they have. Do I make myself clear?"

Celia drew herself up slowly from her chair, "perfectly," she smiled at her friend, "Could we take that last statement as a threat? Definitely not recommended coming from a prospective parent. Won't the judge like to hear all about your timid little mouse of a wife, the money you used to fix this place up, and, of course, your temper." She walked to the door, "I'll leave now, such a ... rewarding ...visit. I'll be back," she promised, and unsmiling walked out the door. Her lawyer friend followed in her wake.

Murphy stood, his hands clenched at his side, the knuckles showing white as he forced himself to let them go. Beth touched the taunt arm, "The children are waiting," she reminded him quietly. Her eyes and face showing the strain and shock of the last few minutes. Murphy looked at Beth's white face, her eyes were enormous hazel pools.

"I'm all right, Beth. That woman is out for blood, mine. She really doesn't care who she hurts in the process. The kids... you. I'm sorry." he said simply.

"I know," Beth whispered, more upset by the news about Joanna than any of Celia's other words. Jealousy was a feeling she had never experienced, never having fallen in love. But hatred and jealousy had coursed through her body at the knowledge that Murphy had been in love with Mike and Jenny's mother. With the pain came the knowledge that she would give anything to have Murphy's love as Joanna had. The greatest shock of all was in realizing that she had fallen in love with her husband, a man in love with his brother's wife. Somehow Beth thought, I can't let him know. We're friends, nothing more she repeated over and over. She forced a smile to her lips, "Let's show them the surprise," she held out a trembling hand to him. He took it gently, firmly, and together they walked to where Casey waited.

Mike's eyes grew enormous as he saw the tiny bundle of fur patiently waiting by his new doghouse. "For us?" he whispered. He tentatively put out a small hand, the puppy responded by licking the fingers one by one. Mike laughed and ran his fingers through her soft brown hair. "I've never had a dog before, what's his name?"

Beth knelt down beside the little boy and wiggling puppy. "He's your dog, you and Jenny must name him. You must also take care of him. Will you do that for us?"

"Oh yes," Mike assured her, solemnly. "His name" he announced after a moment's hesitation, "is Dusty. Cause he's all brown like dust," he went on to explain. "Look Jenny," he said, "isn't he something grand?"

Jenny nodded and stretched out a hand to stroke the tiny ears. At about the same time a purring twosome decided all the attention was going to the wrong subject. Jenny looked down in amazement as Hansel and Gretel walked around her legs, purring, rubbing their backs against her. She forgot the puppy, she stooped and stroked the ginger colored Hansel, and then the cream and white Gretel.

"Hansel and Gretel," Beth explained. "Gretel is going to have kittens. Will you help us take care of them Jenny?" she asked.

Jenny nodded, content to touch the soft hair of the feline. She looked up at Murphy, a small smile touched the corners of her mouth. Murphy bent down, he held her face in the cup of his hand, "You're welcome, Jenny," he whispered to the little girl.

Happiness and pain stabbed at Beth's heart. Happiness that Jenny had responded to the kitten and to Murphy, but a dull pain of sadness that when Murphy looked at Jenny, he wasn't seeing Jenny at all but the lovely Joanna instead.

"Bedtime," Beth announced. "You can play with your new fiends tomorrow. Okay?"

She herded them in, washed them up, and tucked them into bed. Mike held a toy soldier in each hand as he fell asleep. Jenny had a Raggedy Ann and Andy doll in each arm, but in her hand lay a tiny wooden cat that Casey had made.

Beth tiptoed down the hall. Exhaustion finally taking its toll, the dishes she thought. Well, better get started now. When she opened the kitchen door, she stopped in amazement. For there, leaning over the sink was Casey, carefully washing the last pan. Beside him stood Murphy, drying each one as he finished them. They turned as they heard Beth enter. Her eyes filled with tears at the thoughtfulness of the two men. As she hugged Casey and murmured her thanks, he spoke gruffly, "It's the least we could do, you do for us all the time," and hurriedly left.

Beth turned to Murphy, the disarray of her newfound feelings making her suddenly shy. "Don't I get a hug too?" Murphy asked gently," After all, I did dry."

Beth laughed and reached to hug him too, only to find his arms around her as well. In surprise, Beth looked up to question him. His lips found hers in a gentle, soothing kiss. His mouth firm and tender on hers. Beth's hand went to touch his hair, her body curving invitingly against his. The kiss deepened at her response. Slowly, trembling they drew away from each other. Murphy's breathing was harsh, as his chest rose only inches from Beth's face. Her whole body felt abandoned now that she was no longer in his arms.

"Goodnight, Murphy," Beth whispered, as she turned and walked to the door.

"Goodnight, Beth," he said. He remained in the kitchen long after he watched her leave the room.

CHAPTER 8

Beth was awakened by a gentle shake from Murphy next morning, still half asleep she gave him a dreamy smile, "Morning," she murmured. She raised her hand to run through his hair but stopped midway as realization hit her. She dropped her hand, opened her eyes and stared into the warm blue of Murphy's.

"Time to get up, sleepyhead, I'm going to take a shower...Beth, are you alright? ... "he asked concerned with how pale she suddenly seemed.

"Fine," she answered. "Just not used to being awakened by a man that's all."

Murphy gave her a smile that lit up his eyes, "I'm very glad to hear that," he said, his warm glance sending a blush down her neck. He confused her even more by kissing her quickly on the forehead before he went whistling from the room. As he shut the door behind him, Beth jumped up to get her clothes. She quickly made her bed and the small one in the dressing room that Murphy used. She touched his pillow lovingly as she straightened his few belongings. She had just returned to her room when he came from his shower, his hair damp.

"Breakfast in twenty minutes," Beth said as she brushed against him to walk through the door all too conscious of the very masculine smell of his body, the strength in his arms and legs.

Breakfast over, Beth cleaned the kitchen. Threw a load of clothes in the washer and ran the sweeper before she heard the children stir. Going up the stairs, she stopped as she saw both of them coming down the hall. Jenny in another dress of ruffles and lace, Mike in a tan suit. Beth looked at the children.

"Don't you look pretty this morning Jenny, and Mike you look absolutely smashing. But aren't you a little worried about getting your beautiful clothes all dirty?"

They both looked down at their clothes and then back at Beth's jeans and summer blouse. Mike cleared his throat, "These are the only kind of clothes Aunt Celia let us wear. We don't have anything else. We used to," he said wistfully, "But when we went to live with her, she said she wasn't going to be seen dead with us in those clothes." Tears came to his eyes, "We don't want anybody dead anymore."

Beth reached out and hugged the two, "Course not, love. Now I'll tell you what, we'll go shopping. You can pick out the clothes you'll wear, if you want suits, fine, if you want jeans, fine, Okay?"

Two dark heads nodded, "Good, let's go. I've got bacon and eggs this morning."

Cracking the eggs minutes later, Beth tried to catch a glimpse of Murphy out the window. I need to let him know where we're going. She saw him then, walking towards the barn, giving orders to the men unloading the livestock. He was so sure of himself she thought. Oh Murphy, how am I to live with you loving you as I do? The eggs done, she dished out their breakfasts. While they ate, she made a salad and checked to see they had enough chicken and shortcake left for a cold lunch.

"Good," she said as they finished," now let's run upstairs and see what you have and make a list of what you think you'll need."

Unpacking the suitcases, Beth was amazed at the money that had been spent in the fancy clothes for both Jenny and Mike. She made their beds and then they headed for the door. "Mike, you and Jenny had better leave some milk for the cats and Dusty. We don't want them to be thirsty while we're gone, do we?" The children were in instant agreement as they carefully carried the small bowls outside. "You can pet them for a minute while I tell Uncle Murphy where we're going. Mike," she stressed, "stay right here in the yard."

Beth ran towards the barn, "Murphy," she called, "Murphy!"

He emerged and gave her a surprised look. "What's wrong? Is it one of the kids?"

"No, at least not in that way. I'm taking the kids to town. All Mike has are three-piece suits and Jenny has ruffles and lace, they need play clothes, jeans, and shirts, tennis shoes," she watched Murphy set his face into grin lines. "Is it all right if I go?" she asked. "You don't mind?"

"Take them, buy what they need," he said crisply. "How could anyone not have brought play clothes for living on a farm," he exploded. "Doesn't she remember what it's like to be a kid?"

Beth said quietly, "Lunch is in the refrigerator. I'll be back as soon as I can." She turned to go, Murphy caught her swiftly, pulled her to him and kissed her. His arms seemed to enfold her, as he drank the sweetness of her kiss.

As he reluctantly let her go, he brushed the top of her hair with his lips and murmured, "Thanks Beth, for being as you are." He straightened and grinned, his anger gone, "and don't spend too much money!"

Beth hurried back to Mike and Jenny still a bit dazed at Murphy's kiss. Mike was sitting in the grass, a contented puppy sleeping in his lap. Jenny was actually laughing as the two cats wound themselves around her legs, their tails tickling her knees. "Ready?" she asked the children. "If we hurry," Beth added as she saw their disappointment at leaving their new pets, "we'll stop at the pet shop and you can each get a surprise for Dusty and Hansel and Gretel."

Smiles spread on their faces as they ran to the car. On the way she named the places they needed to go to in the Mall, all those shops would surely have what she needed. She parked, took Jenny by the hand and gave Mike her other one and walked in. It was huge, over 60 stores under a huge dome. In the middle was a fountain, with padded benches for the weary travelers. Flowers grew everywhere, almost as if you were outside. The children were in awe of the bustling people and the stores that seemed to be lined up forever. Checking the directory, Beth took the children up the escalator, and turned to find the "Children's Shop." Once there she knew she had come to the right place. Watching the faces of Mike and Jenny, she wandered around the store until a saleslady approached her. "May I help you?"

"Yes," Beth answered, "Mike needs some blue jeans. I'm not sure of the size, can he try them on, and wear a pair home?"

"Certainly, miss. Come right this way."

"Jenny," Beth turned to her, "Do you want jeans too?" A shy nod followed. "We'll need some for her, too." Beth informed the saleslady.

"Mike," Beth called out, "how about some T-shirts that say Superman?" She heard Mike's "Wow" even outside the door. She smiled, what darlings, pretending just for a moment that Mike and Jenny were really hers and Murphy's. Two different children came out of the store. Both wearing jeans and T-shirts, Mike's had a picture of Superman; Jenny's had a small kitten on it.

"Now shoes," Beth said, as she juggled the packages while holding onto the two small hands. Shoes were a different matter. "They could sit down at least," Beth thought. Mike chose navy with white strips down the sides, Jenny chose pale blue with pictures of cartoon characters on them. Again, Beth asked if they could wear them home.

Putting some under her arm, the rest she held in her hand, she took Jenny in her other hand, and asked Mike to hold onto Jenny's. "This way," Beth told them, and minutes later both let go and ran happily into the Pet Shop. Mike decided on a collar and a rubber ball, "Dusty can learn to do tricks," he said. Jenny pointed to two small collars and a box of Cat Nip.

Happily, they carried the bundles to the car.

"How about lunch? Are you hungry? Do you like hamburgers and French fries?" Mike's exuberant, "Yeah!" and Jenny's smile decided Beth to try the nearest quick food hamburger restaurant.

As they turned into the lane, Mike and Jenny were no longer the quiet, subdued children they had been when they arrived. Two denim clad figures raced from the car to show their new clothes to Casey and Murphy as they stood by the back porch, then off to their pets. Casey and Murphy watched as they ran and jumped with Dusty.

Very softly, Murphy whispered in her ear as he took the packages from her hands, "You've done it again."

Beth looked back questioningly, "Done what?"

"First you took a ransacked farm and turned it into a showplace, then you take two statues and change them into real live children, what's next?" He queried as he watched a soft blush of pleasure cross her cheeks.

"Two's my quota," she stammered, alarmed at the way her body was reacting to the nearness of him.

"I doubt it," Murphy grinned. "I doubt it! I'm beginning to think I married a witch. Capturing hearts wherever she goes, Casey's your devoted slave. Father Mac is under your thumb. You should have heard Luke singing your praise when he delivered that hay. Is there anybody not under that spell?"

Only you, Beth thought longingly. But she answered quickly, "Celia?" and looked up to find Murphy watching her intently.

"How about a date?" Murphy asked bluntly.

"What?" said a completely confused Beth, "Why?"

"You've worked hard these past weeks. You need a break. Besides I want to get to know you better," he said. Beth's heart skipped a beat at what his words could mean.

"What about Mike and Jenny?" She asked.

"Casey will watch them, will you go out with your husband, ...friend?" Murphy was suddenly very serious, "Please... "

Beth gave a radiant smile, "I'd love to, friend." she answered simply. "When?"

97

Murphy let out a long sigh, almost as if he'd been holding his breath waiting for her answer. "Tomorrow is Saturday night, we'll catch an early movie, dinner afterwards, you might even talk me into dancing. Sound alright?"

"You don't sound like your usual domineering self," Beth laughed.

"Domineering?" Murphy asked.

"Right, the man I married would have said, We'll leave at 4:35, Movie starts at 5:30, Dinner at 8:00, Dancing at 9:00, Home by 11:00!" She mimicked, at his puzzled expression, "Don't you remember, in Uncle Henry's office how you gave me the wedding plans!"

Murphy's face creased in laughter, "I didn't know you then, I only saw your eyes, fighting mad they were. I thought it best to squash any resistance right then. Only it didn't work, if my memory serves, you just got sassier. Ah yes, Sir. I wondered how I would ever be able to live with such a little spitfire."

"You've survived," Beth said. "Has it been that bad?"

"I don't want you to get a big head, I'll tell you later." He kissed her nose teasingly. "Let's go Casey," and he headed off towards the barn whistling as he went.

Late that night Beth woke to the crying of someone. Donning on her robe, she hurried down the hall, Jenny's door was open. Mike knelt on the floor by Jenny's bed trying to help the sobbing little girl. "Oh Jenny," Beth whispered, "What's wrong love," she crooned, as she gathered the shaking form to her. Turning to Mike she saw tears down his cheeks, too. "Come on, Mike, there's room for you, too." Both children cuddled up to her and

98

Beth rocked slowly back and forth, talking softly as she rocked.

Her talking soothed them, she hummed, singing softly hoping not to wake up Murphy. Slowly they calmed down, both snuggling up to her warm body. At last they slept, but now Beth was afraid to move least she wake them. Her cramped muscles making sleep impossible. She tried to shift Jenny to relieve her already numb arm, but her whimpering made Beth stop.

"Hush, love," Beth crooned. "It's all right, go to sleep ..."

A shadow over the bed, caused her to look up, her heart quickening. As she saw Murphy a deep breath escaped her. "Beth," he whispered, "what's wrong? Are they sick?"

Beth shook her head, "Homesick, frightened, feeling terribly unhappy and not really knowing who to turn to or what to do." she said softly. "Poor darlings. "

Murphy gently picked up Mike and carried him to his own bed. When he returned, Beth was able to slip from the tightly held clasp of Jenny's and eased herself from the bed. Careful not to disturb the tiny child in the bed. As she went to stand, her legs, numb from the cramped position, refused to hold Beth's weight. Murphy caught her, strong arms held her, as they regained their feeling, keeping her from falling. Beth was overwhelmingly aware of his bare chest, the hard feel of his body, his lean rippling muscles pressed close to her. She was aware of a longing beginning in the deep hollows of her body, a desperate ache to feel his lips on her, to feel those hands on her body. Knowing she had to get away quickly before she betrayed her feelings, Beth pushed against his chest and stepped backwards.

Murphy quickly released her, at Beth's softly whispered words, "I'm alright now, thanks." She felt suddenly bereft without his arms.

They walked quietly from the room, down the hall and to their own bedroom. Beth was all too conscious of his presence, following in her wake. Once inside their room, she walked to the bed, feeling very vulnerable. Afraid her thoughts were as transparent as the clamoring of her body's desires. Murphy walked slowly to the dressing room, Beth's voice stopped him at the door, "I'm sorry we woke you."

"You didn't," he uttered. "I woke feeling something was wrong, I got up to check and noticed your bed empty, I was worried you might have been ill."

"Goodnight, Murphy," Beth whispered as she climbed into bed once more hoping sleep would claim her, dulling the pain of loving Murphy.

The morning started as usual, the thought of an evening with Murphy bringing a slight blush to her cheeks, a shine to her eyes. She sang as she prepared the sausage and pancakes, jumping as the phone rang, Murphy rose from the table. His cheerful "Hello," changed abruptly as he quickly handed the phone to a surprised Beth. His face was set, a nerve in the side of his jaw jumped.

"Hello," Beth answered nervously, wondering who it could be that could change Murphy so quickly.

"Beth, love," the familiar voice said.

"Johnny" Beth exclaimed; the thoughts of Murphy's anger momentarily pushed aside at the sound of his voice. "It's great to hear from you!"

"Is that why I wasn't invited to the wedding?" Johnny asked. The teasing in his voice only slightly masking the seriousness of his question.

"Johnny, you know I love you," Beth began unaware of the effect her words had on the man standing behind her. "Murphy just swept me off my feet and we were married before I had a chance to tell anyone." She forced a laugh, "Now I'm an old married woman with two kids ..."

Johnny's voice broke in, "Well just as long as you live happily ever after. Is he treating you right, luv?"

"I'm fine Johnny," Beth assured him, "How's the music corning?"

"Pretty good," he retorted, "Although having lost my best girl and singer, it could be worse! Listen luv, I have to catch a plane, I just wanted to give you my best and let you know if you need me, call me."

"Thanks, Johnny. I'll remember," Beth said softly, "take care." She hung up and turned to find Murphy watching her with an intentness that gave Beth a start. "That was Johnny," Beth began, "my pianist, I told you about him ..."

"About tonight," Murphy interrupted her abruptly, "We'd better cancel." At her questioning stare, Murphy went on, "the nightmares might return to the kids. We'll make it some other time."

Beth was astonished at the coldness of his words, she could only nod. "If you think that's best ..."

"I do," he affirmed. He walked to the door, and with a cool nod to Casey, he left.

Beth's bewilderment at his attitude left her standing, staring after him. What have I done? Could he see how she felt about him? Oh God, how am I to get through the next few months, she thought. Wearily she leaned against the wall, allowing her composure to break and wept silently for the broken promise of what might have been.

Murphy's cold, unresponsive attitude towards Beth continued. He was polite, but the easy teasing banter they once had shared was gone. He spent long days working the fields and caring for the animals. He did manage time to play with the children. With them his indifference would fade. He laughed, he was gentle, and he was patient. Listening to Mike's chatter, coaxing the silent Jenny to open up, he was the Murphy Beth had been allowed to glimpse.

The strain of Murphy's rejection began to show on Beth. She lost weight. The nights seemed endless as she tossed and turned, listening for Murphy's even breathing, so close and yet so far. Beth ached for his touch. Since the morning, he had cancelled their date, Murphy avoided any personal touch with Beth, no more casual kisses, no friendly pat on the shoulder. It was as if for Murphy she failed to exist except as a housekeeper to the children and as a cook for them all.

Dark shadows began to appear beneath her eyes, her clothes hung on her, sometimes even her smile seemed forced. Casey watched her with guarded, worried eyes. Several times he mentioned his worry to Beth, but she would give him a smile that didn't quite reach her eyes and a quick kiss on his cheek. "I'm fine, don't worry about me," and quickly change the subject. He then mentioned her to Murphy only to be told to mind his own business. His temper was easily aroused these days. He was abrupt to the point of rudeness.

Only when they were with the children did he relax. Around Jenny and Mike, they had an unspoken agreement to behave as normally as possible. Under this normalcy, Mike blossomed, he was an active, inquisitive boy. He spent his days running with Dusty through the fields, climbing the orchards in search of early apples, making a clubhouse of straw in the barn, and catching tadpoles in Piasa Creek. He adored Beth and hung on Murphy's every word, but it was Casey who became his confidante. Casey always had time to listen, his hands never still, molding, whittling. Mike followed him about the farm, taking Casey's words as gospel.

Jenny laughed at Dusty's antics, she played with Hansel and Gretel, and followed Beth about the house. She could sleep through the night, but she would not talk. Murphy would hold her on his lap, read her stories, gently tuck her into bed, but it was to Beth that Jenny turned. She followed Beth as she cleaned, a silent shadow. Beth would carry on a quiet conversation with her, waiting for her nod, singing softly as they did the chores. Jenny would touch her hair, kiss her cheek. Sometimes she would hum with Beth, carefully holding one or more of her dolls, or more often just sitting, petting a contented Gretel on her lap.

Time passed slowly as the days stretched into weeks. Beth visited Father Mac and Miss Lucy frequently taking the children with her. Both worried about the change they saw in Beth. The hopeless bewilderment they saw in her eyes. Miss Lucy's visits followed a pattern. She now lived with her nieces and as the children played with her great nieces, Beth would chat with her telling her of their progress, listening to Miss Lucy tell of the past, then Beth would go to the old piano that sat in the corner of the room and play all the songs Miss Lucy wanted to hear. Beth would sometimes lose herself in her songs, forgetting the quiet figure sitting in the rocker. She sang the old ballads, the hymns from church, her voice brought tears to Miss Lucy's eyes, so vibrant and sweet the melodious sound.

"What's wrong child? What's making you so sad?" Miss Lucy asked her as she finished singing.

Her plea right after the singing pierced through the wall of defense and Beth crumbled. Great sobs racked her body as she knelt by Miss Lucy's knees. "Oh, Miss Lucy ...he doesn't love me. Sometimes I feel...he...doesn't even like me. He's so unapproachable." She wept, her eyes wide and overflowing as the dam holding her was broken. "He's built a wall. I can't reach him. He married me to get the children. I love him so... I don't know what to do."

Miss Lucy held her, soothed her hair, "Hush, child, it's all right. I know Murphy. Listen now to an old woman." Beth wiped her eyes, giving a great sniff as she tried to regain her composure. "When you first came, did Murphy treat you coldly?"

Beth shook her head. "When I first met Murphy he was, but on the way here we decided we could be friends." She sighed a deep sigh that seemed to come from her very soul. "He was so different. We would laugh and talk. He would just show up to tell me something, other times just to see what I was doing." Her forehead creased with the effort to remember. "He had asked me out. We were going to dinner, a show. I got up early as usual, then right after breakfast, he just said we'd make it some other time. He's been aloof ever since."

"Did anything happen at breakfast, Beth? Or what about the night before? Think, love, can you recall anything that was said or done?" Miss Lucy's voice was calm but searching as she looked for some clue that could explain Murphy's behavior.

"I do remember I was up with Jenny and Mike that night. Nightmares, crying, Murphy found me there and helped put the children back in their beds. But he wasn't cold then, he seemed to understand their tears," Beth spoke softly.

"Now the morning, Beth," Miss Lucy persisted, "did you have any visitors, calls, anything at all?"

Beth shook her head, "No, I don't think so... No, wait, Johnny called. But I didn't talk long, he's my ...pianist," she explained to Miss Lucy.

"Does Murphy know Johnny?" Miss Lucy asked shrewdly.

"They've never met. Johnny just called to make sure I was alright. He's looked after me for years, he's a very good friend," she went on to explain to Miss Lucy. "We've been through so much together. He was teasing me about getting married without telling him." Beth gave a wry smile, "I told him I was very happy and not to worry, I still loved him."

A shrewd, pleased smile covered Miss Lucy's face, "He's jealous," she stated boldly. Total surprise was Beth's response.

She shook her head slowly, "Oh, no, Miss Lucy," she cried sadly, "you have to care for someone to be jealous and Murphy," she swallowed, "doesn't care that way about me."

"Correction," said Miss Lucy, "he's never said he cares about you. He cares. I've seen the way he avoids looking at you now. If he didn't care, he wouldn't have changed. He's hurt, jealous, probably feels the old hurt."

Beth's questioning look held confusion.

"Did you know that Joanna, Marshall's wife used to be Murphy's fiancé?"

"Yes, Celia told me the first night we had dinner with the children when they arrived. I'm sure that Murphy sees Joanna every time he looks at Jenny, thinking that she could be his own daughter. Instead, he's stuck with me..."

"Now hold on child, don't go drawing conclusions before you know the whole story. You know Murphy played football, he used to have girls, women, falling all over him. Then, he met Joanna. She was a beautiful, young thing. A lot different than Celia, but alike in that she usually got what she wanted. She liked Murphy and the spotlight and, of course, the money he was making. He in turn liked Joanna. I say 'liked' because if he had loved her, he never would have let her go, even for his brother. Anyway, Murphy must have decided it was time to settle down. Joanna accepted. Then came the accident. Murphy was scarred, no more football and no more big bucks. During it all Marshall was there, and Joanna and Marshall spent a lot of time together. When Murphy got back on his feet, things had changed. This time Joanna was in love with Marshall, of course, and it was love, for little brother had no money. They told Murphy finally and just as they were growing up, Marshall got what he wanted and Murphy took the flack, and there was plenty. The press had a heyday. Murphy being dumped because of his scars! Murphy driving her away in his fury! Younger brother takes all! It was a mess. Whether Murphy really believed any of it, I don't know, but he did do his hermit act. The next we heard he was married to you."

"Miss Lucy," Beth began, "how does this explain his reaction to me?"

"Don't you see, Beth," she explained patiently, "he had started caring about you too when he overheard your conversation with this Johnny. He's decided the only way not to be hurt again is to steer clear of you."

Beth shook her head skeptically, but Miss Lucy's explanation had planted a seed of hope.

CHAPTER 9

Returning home from Miss Lucy's, Beth was in a very pensive mood, thoughts of Murphy interrupting her train of explanations. Pulling into the lane, she noticed a strange car in the driveway. The children saw it, too.

"Aunt Celia," Mike spoke stonily. Jenny moved closer to Beth. "Does ... this mean we have to go back with her?" he asked dejectedly.

Beth's look of complete surprise at his remark, caused her to look closely at the two small waifs waiting patiently for her answer. "Mike, Jenny... "she began, "Your uncle Murphy and I...we love you and want more than anything else for you to be happy. Do you want to go back with Aunt Celia?"

Two small dark heads shook their answers emphatically. Two pairs of deep blue eyes grew larger and expectant as Beth finished speaking, "Well then, why should we send you with her? We want you here with us, all the time... forever Mike." She stopped the car as four small arms hugged her neck in a delicious stranglehold of relief and love. As Beth opened the door, glowing from their hugs, she was met by the angry eyes of Celia.

Dressed to kill, thought Beth, as she surveyed the glittering black jumpsuit that clung to Celia's voluptuous figure, leaving little to the imagination as the neckline plunged to almost her waist. "Where have you been?" demanded Celia. "I have been waiting for almost 30 minutes."

Beth remained calm, sending the children on ahead to play with their pets. "Celia, had you called and let us know you were corning, we would have been here. We were out visiting friends."

Her calmness only infuriated Celia more. "Why did you send them off? I came to visit them, are you going to try to keep them from me?" Celia's voice raised higher.

Beth saw Murphy approaching from the barn, his face already set in uncompromising lines as he heard Celia's voice.

"No Celia, we're not," Beth replied swiftly, "but if you really came to see the children, be my guests, they're playing with their pets in the back yard." Beth felt Murphy's presence even before she felt his hand on her shoulder. She turned her face up to him, trying to give him a welcoming smile that things were under control. But too many feelings were churning in her mind, her smile trembled softly. She felt his hand tighten on her shoulder, and his lips gently brushed hers.

Beth's heart swelled at Murphy's response, his first since the telephone call. Now Beth's smile turned tremulous, her eyes glowed. Murphy touched her nose with his finger, tracing its pert curve. He gave her a warm smile in return.

Celia's harsh voice vibrated through the air, "Excuse me. Don't let my presence or that of the children put a damper on your love life."

Murphy turned to face Celia, his voice remained calm, his eyes glinted dangerously. "The children are never an unwelcome interruption. What brings you out this time, Celia? More mud to sling or you just don't want us to live happily ever after, the wicked witch returns?"

Celia's laughter was brittle as she took a step forward, "But that would make you the handsome prince. And we all know you're no Prince Charming, not with that face."

"Do we?" Beth asked softly. "I think he makes a perfect knight in shining armor come to protect me from ..." she paused, "The wicked dragons in the forest." Her arms moved around Murphy's waist, she let her head rest on his shoulder, she heard his breath quicken. "If you came to see the kids," Beth added, "do so, but don't make any more comments about my husband, or you will no longer be welcome here." Her sincerity was unquestionable. Her words, while spoken softly, held a wealth of meaning.

Celia turned on her heel and headed for the back yard. Her fury seemed to leave a trail in her wake as she kicked at the rocks that bordered the walkway.

Murphy turned Beth so she was facing him. His hand came under her chin and forced her to look up at him. Now embarrassed by her remark to Celia, Beth stubbornly refused to meet his eyes.

"Beth, look at me," he asked softly. When she shook her head, Murphy kissed her, not the gentle kiss she knew before, but a kiss that seemed to go on and on. His arms held her; his tongue explored the sweetness of her lips. As they parted Murphy plundered into their dark depths. Beth's hands clutched at Murphy's shirt as an ecstasy and wonder filled her body. On its own, her soft hips molded to his hard thighs.

Finally, Murphy raised his head, breathing heavily, he said again softly, "Beth, look at me."

Beth raised her eyes to him, trembling from his kiss.

"Why did you defend me to Celia?" he whispered. His hands moving sensuously over her back. "Beth?"

"I just ... "Beth began and ran her tongue over the tip of her lips, unaware of how provocative she looked, "I just couldn't listen to her trying to belittle you. It's not fair. I didn't mean to embarrass you; I just can't let her hurt you." Beth's voice dropped to a barely audible murmur. Her eyes closed afraid of the anger she was sure she'd find in Murphy's eyes.

"Thank you, Beth," he said, his voice was husky, low filled with an emotion Beth could not define. She raised her eyes, relieved to find he wasn't angry.

"You didn't mind?" Beth asked incredulously.

"Mind?! Mind?! You are the first person who has ever tried to protect me." His voice held a touch of awe. He looked at her face cupped now in his large hands. A shout from the yard broke into their private world. Murphy kissed her again, causing her knees to feel weak. "Go rescue our kids," he told her, "and Beth," she took a step away from him and looked at him. He took a ragged breath, "can we make a date? This one we'll keep."

Beth's eyes grew soft and her smile brought the dimple to her cheek, "Oh, yes," she agreed happily, "I'd like that very much." She walked away, her feet barely touching the ground as she hurried to the back yard to join Celia, Mike and Jenny. Leaving Murphy watched her even after she was gone from sight. Beth found a tearful

Jenny standing between Gretel and Celia, while Mike held Dusty in his arms, his face belligerent as he faced his Aunt. As they saw Beth, Mike called her name.

"What's wrong, love?" Beth asked alarmed by the tension she felt.

"She said they had fleas and that she'd make you get rid of them." Mike turned imploring eyes to Beth's, "Will you, Aunt Beth?"

"Mike," Beth assured both children, "those pets are yours, your aunt will not hurt them or take them away. Your uncle Murphy wouldn't let her, and neither would Casey or I."

The children turned triumphant faces at Celia, content in the knowledge that no one could harm their pets.

"Jenny, Mike...why don't you get some milk for them." She smiled as Jenny reluctantly left Gretel, "She needs the milk for her babies, Jenny. We want them born healthy, don't we?"

Jenny nodded happily as thoughts of little kittens came to mind. She skipped merrily after the disappearing figure of Mike.

"How dare you!" Celia exploded. "What gives you the right to give those miserable animals to my niece and nephew? Or to undermine my authority." she sneered as Beth refused to be intimidated. "You little tramp. if you think that simply by marrying Murphy you can tell me what to do, you had better think again. Just because he gives you a kiss don't feel you can replace my sister, as his lover or their mother. You are nothing, and I won't allow them to be raised by you or him."

"I think you had better go," Beth said, an underlying note of steel creeping into the words.

"I'm going!" Celia said threateningly, "But I'll be back."

Beth watched as she walked to her car and sped off down the lane.

"Is she gone?" Mike asked from the kitchen door. Beth's answering grin had him scooting out the door, followed by his sister carefully balancing a bowl of milk. A contented Gretel lapped the liquid, Jenny watched her patiently.

Beth leaned down to touch her hair, as she looked up, Beth spoke gently, "Better start thinking about names for those kittens, love, it won't be long now. In fact," she assured the shining wide blue eyes, "you'd better find a box and put some old rags in it, just for when she's ready!"

Hearing someone whistling, she turned, hoping it was Murphy. Seeing the bent form of Casey, Beth's heart slowed, she gave him a tremulous smile.

"Hello, Miss Beth, Missy," he addressed Jenny. "I came up to let you know I'll be glad to watch the young 'uns tonight. And don't you go worrying about feeding us. I'll cook up some soup and we'll make some 'Casey Special's.' You and Mr. Murphy just have a good time."

"Oh Casey!" Beth cried, and she leaned over and kissed the gnarled cheek. "You are wonderful, are you sure?"

His face reddened, "Course I'm sure," he mumbled as he walked away, his fingers going up to gently touch his cheek where Beth's kiss had been.

"Tonight!" Beth thought. Oh Murphy! I love you so! Will I ever be able to tell you? Running inside she ran up the stairs wondering as she went what she could wear.

As she gave the children their bath, she thought about their evening. Oh, let everything go all right. No calls, please! If we can just be on our own, we'll be able to go back as we were. Maybe he'll fall in love and we'll live here with Jenny and Mike and our own children ... " Beth blushed as she thought of having Murphy's child in her arms. A slow smile spread across her face as she bundled the two into towels and across the hall to get them dressed, meeting Murphy at the door.

At the sight of her, with her hair in curlers and an old lilac bath robe on, he grinned and asked, "Ready to go?" and dodged her shove as she shut the door.

The children dressed in their pajamas, she ushered them downstairs and hurried to get ready. She pulled the curlers from her hair as Murphy walked in. His hair damp from the shower, his powerful shoulders glistening, he exuded such an overwhelming magnetism Beth gripped the curlers to keep from holding out her hands to welcome him. She could feel his hard body against her, her knuckles showed white as she calmly smiled, glad he could not read her thoughts or know the power he had over her body, her soul.

"Better hurry," he said as he passed, leaving Beth breathing a deep sigh. She hurriedly ran a brush through the fine brown hair, glad that for once it was managing to curl as she wanted it to and not as haphazardly as it usually did. Taking off her robe revealed her slip and underclothes, as she slipped the apricot silk sheath over her head, she hoped her choice would please Murphy. Smoothing the folds of the simple cut dress, revealing the soft womanly curves of her firm young breasts, the slight waist, and shapely hips which met her long, lithe legs she reached to zip it, only to have it stick halfway.

As she worked on the zipper, Murphy walked in. "Need some help?"

Beth caught her breath, in evening clothes Murphy was devastatingly handsome. "Yes," she said, "my zipper is stuck."

Beth trembled as Murphy's hands touched her skin. She could feel the warmth emanating from his body. Slowly Murphy zipped up the dress, his hands lingering on her neck, he felt the golden silkiness of her skin, breathed in deeply of the scent of her hair. He bent his head and whispered, "You are so beautiful," as he kissed the velvet softness of her skin. "Yes, I find you very beautiful. From the top of your head to the tips of your toes, and believe me," he smiled, "I know a beautiful woman when I see one. Didn't you know I was a connoisseur?" Trying to lighten the suddenly charged atmosphere between them.

Beth took her cue, "Oh dear. That must be from your sordid X-rated past," she teased.

"Well, you know, sordid X-rated pasts are a perfect foil for beautiful women," he quipped.

"Maybe I should have been in your past then," Beth retorted gaily.

"Not you," Murphy was suddenly serious, "you are the beautiful woman of my present. Shall we go?"

And future please, Beth wished silently as they walked to the door.

They kissed the children goodnight, wished Casey luck and headed to the car. Beth felt suddenly carefree and lighthearted as she felt Murphy's hand on her arm as he helped her in. A teasing banter between them was kept up to the theater, and a lively, unpredictable comedy followed. Beth was very aware of Murphy, his shoulder brushing hers, his warm clasp of her hand, the hearty sound of his laugh.

Oh Murphy, Beth thought, I love you more each day. How am I to leave you at the end of the year. Beth took a deep breath, take each day as it comes, she told herself. Treasure each moment as it arrives, later when you're gone, each memory will be that much sweeter. Having resolved to enjoy each moment with Murphy, Beth laughed lovingly up at his face as the show progressed.

Murphy was enjoying himself; the show was good he thought but it felt very right to be sitting next to Beth. He listened to her delightful contagious laugh, the corners of her mouth curving upwards. She looks happy, he thought, happy to be with me. A thrust of pride made him breathe deeply, it had been a long time since anyone had been interested in him, his feelings. He thought back to earlier when she had tried to protect him, a deep contentment filled his mind as a deep longing entered his heart to keep her, possess her as thoughts of her gentleness possessed him.

When the show ended, Murphy led Beth to the car holding her small delicate hand firmly in his own much larger one. They were quiet on the way to the restaurant, both content in the easy silence. A table for two had been reserved and they were rushed to it by a very solemn head waiter.

"I don't know what to order," Beth confessed wryly, "everything sounds so good."

"Maybe because you don't have to cook it." Murphy added.

Beth laughed, the dimple appearing in her cheeks. "Probably, but I never cook these fancy dishes, so it's not a fair comparison. What delectable morsel do you intend to have?"

"You," Murphy spoke quietly watching the blush rise to her cheeks, the promise of his words causing her to raise startled eyes to his. His face was serious, his dark eyes deep, mysterious, holding a warmth that was unmistakable.

Beth shook off her confusion, "I'd probably give you heartburn," she said. Hoping to mask the feelings of longing she felt.

He smiled, the corners of his mouth twitched, as the waiter came to take their order, "I'll have ... " he paused catching Beth's eye and her breath, "the filet mignon, baked potato, Italian dressing on my salad and we'll also have a bottle of champagne."

The waiter turned to Beth, "the same please," she murmured, still in a state of confusion. Murphy's words echoing in her mind.

The dinner was delicious, the champagne tickled Beth's nose, causing a giggle to form deep in her throat. Her husky laugh was infectious as Murphy watched the wrinkling of her cute nose. As soft music began to play, he wanted to hold her slim body in his arms. He stood, extending a hand to her, she rose putting her hand in his. Her body seemed to melt into his as her feet moved with a mind of their own matching the intricate steps of his. His arms tightened, as he drew her unresisting body closer to his. He could feel the soft pliancy of her, the warmth radiating. His hand moved sensually over her back, causing a tremor to run through her body. Beth closed her eyes, feeling as if she were in heaven. Her head rested against his chest, her hand moving from his shoulder to curl itself in the nap of his hair. She felt his kiss as it touched her hair, a deep ache filled her as her body responded asking for more. A deep sigh came from the depths of Murphy's soul, he whispered huskily into Beth's ear, "Let's go home." She looked up to nod, as she did, Murphy dropped a featherlike kiss on her parted lips. His arms tightened convulsively around her, as he led her from the floor. She waited while he paid the check, her mind dreamily wondering over the evening and the promise of what lay ahead.

Murphy kept his arms protectively around her as they walked to the car. Once inside, he drew the unresisting Beth close to him, a slow thorough kiss had her senses clamoring for more. His breath quickened as he felt her response. He started the car keeping her beside him, her head resting on his shoulder, his arm brushed her breast. Beth felt a warmth steal over her. A deep sigh escaped her as she lay against him. Neither spoke as they drove home. Beth's hand rested lightly on his arm feeling the strength and power beneath the suit he wore. The car drove along the Great River Road. The twinkling of the lights on the barges, and the gentle breeze causing the leaves to sway overhead combined to create an illusion of fairy tale enchantment. Murphy moved his arm to circle her shoulders. His hand moved slowly, rhythmically against her, down her arm. His fingers brushed her breast only to move lingeringly away. He turned into their lane, driving slowly, expertly between the white fences. As he stopped the car, he drew her to him kissing first her eyes, then the tip of her nose, and finally her lips, drawing from Beth a response that she had never felt before. He helped her from the car, keeping his arm caressingly around her.

As they entered the house, a sleepy Casey bid them goodnight as he hurried past. The door closed behind him. Murphy drew her back into his arms, now insistent, drawing her pliant body towards him. Molding her to his. A trembling started in her and she clung to him, returning his passion. His hands moved slowly down her back, unzipping the silkiness that covered her. He slipped the dress from her shoulders, caressing her neck, nibbling her ears. The straps of her slip were lowered revealing the delicate swelling of her breasts, a movement of his hands on her back and her bra was gently removed. His hands touched the velvety softness of her, his arms holding her as his lips lowered to kiss the upturned peaks. A moan escaped Beth's lips as he teased them. Her breasts swelled and rose at his touch. Murphy picked her up in his arms effortlessly, he walked up the stairs and deposited her gently on the bed. His body lowering beside hers. His hands gently removing her clothes, touching the softness of her breasts, moving slowly downwards to the curve of her hip--her thigh. His kisses deepened, leaving Beth wanting more as she returned his kisses, her body seeking the warmth of his hands. Delicious tremors of pleasure arose from his touch, a deep longing. Her fingers unbuttoned his shirt, slipping it down his shoulders. Her hands feeling the rippling muscles beneath her touch, they moved across his chest.

Murphy drew a ragged breath, as he murmured her name, "Do you know what you're doing to me? I want you," he whispered against her lips.

Realization of his words hit Beth abruptly. Not wanting to draw back from his touch she lay quietly. Her face turned to Murphy's shoulder, she whispered silently into it. As he heard her words, his hands stopped their slow exploration. He raised himself on one arm, he lifted Beth's chin with the other. His voice husky with emotion, "What did you say Beth?"

A tremor shot through her body as she looked at the eyes, liquid with emotion and passion. She touched her suddenly dry lips with her tongue, "I said, will you show me what to do...I've never," she paused "...made love before." Her voice dropped to a bare whisper as she looked embarrassingly away from him.

His voice was soft, "You're a virgin."

She nodded; his hands tightened on her chin. "You've never been with a man before." She nodded, swallowing nervously.

Murphy pulled himself away. He covered Beth with the bedspread, his mouth a tight line. He stood up; Beth unconsciously reached for his hand. Her confession causing her to ask "Why?" embarrassed and hurt by his withdrawal.

"I don't make love to virgins." Murphy stated abruptly. "I'm, no celibate but the women I take to bed know the score." His tone softened as he saw the pain his words had caused Beth. "It's best this way. If we had gone on much farther, you would have lost your grounds for divorce and annulment at the end of a year. We said no strings, remember?"

Beth reluctantly shook her head, inside a voice was crying out that was before I fell in love with you. She had pride too, she would not let Murphy see how much she ached for him. She managed a small smile, "Murphy ..." she began, only to stop, trying to find the right words, "Murphy, can we still be friends?"

She held her breath, as Murphy stopped in midstream. Minutes seemed to stretch endlessly as she waited for his reply. A shudder seemed to shake his entire body, his hands clenched tightly at his sides, his knuckles were white. His voice was low, "Oh, Beth ..." he breathed, "We can try" as he walked into his bedroom, Beth thought she heard him add, "but it's not just friends I want to be."

CHAPTER 10

The next few days were long ones for Beth. She was embarrassed by Murphy's withdrawal and hurt by his rejection, and angry at her own response to his touch, angrier still by the fact that if he had shown the slightest inclination to make love to her, she knew she would be powerless to control her wanting him. The nights were unbearable. Beth would lie awake, knowing he was so near yet so far. Memories of how she had responded to his kiss, his caress. She could feel afresh the touch of his hand on her body. A soft moan escaped her as she buried her face in her pillow to stifle her sobs from Murphy.

Two days later an excited Jenny ran into the kitchen where Beth was kneading dough, deciding the best way to get through the next few weeks was to keep as busy as possible. "What is it, love? Do you want me to come with you, all right let me wipe my hands ... "Jenny couldn't wait, she grabbed one of Beth's hands and dragged her outside, almost colliding into Murphy at the door?

"Where's the fire, Jenny?" he asked as she took hold of his hand, too. "What's Up?" he asked Beth, smiling. "I've never seen her so excited!"

Shaking her head, Beth returned his smile. "I really don't know, unless...Jenny, is it Gretel?"

Jenny turned a radiant smile at them, nodding her dark head, causing her pigtails to bob. At the shed, she carefully opened the door. Inside the box Jenny had very lovingly made, purred a contented Gretel and four tiny mewing balls of fur.

Beth and Jenny dropped to their knees. "Oh, Jenny," Beth breathed reaching to pet the head of Gretel. The four tiny kittens snuggled up to Gretel searching for her warmth and security, each showing its own individuality even at this early stage.

The largest was a miniature illusion of Hansel. A soft ginger, the smallest was all white except for one cream colored ear. The remaining two were a combination of ginger, cream, and white creating a calico patchwork on their backs; one had a cream-colored tail, the other was ginger. Gretel seemed quite proud and very motherly as she washed each kitten with tiny licks from her coarse tongue.

Murphy spoke softly bending down to look at the box full of life and the faces of Beth and Jenny, "They're beautiful, Jenny. What do you think you'll be naming them?" A pregnant silence followed, as Beth and Murphy waited, hoping that Jenny would talk. At long last, Murphy sighed,

"You think about it, okay, and when you come up with just the right names, let us know?"

Jenny shook her head, deep in thought unaware of the disappointing look shared by Murphy and Beth. Beth broke the silence, "Have you shown Mike and Casey? Jenny? No? Well off you go then" As she turned, "Thank you for sharing this with us."

As she skipped joyfully off, Beth walked to the door. Murphy's hand stopped her, his fingers gently caressing as they touched her arm.

"Don't be disappointed Beth. She'll talk yet."

"I know, it's just ... I feel so useless trying to help her. I just wish there was something I could do."

"Do?" Murphy echoed incredulously, "Do? You do more for Jenny than anyone would ever expect from her own mother. You love her. You understand her, there's nothing else you can do except give her time." He touched her cheek with his finger, wiping away a solitary tear. Wordlessly they stared at each other, as time stood still. Her body swayed forward, her lips parted, Murphy's head bent down to touch her lightly on the lips, then crushed her to him, his kiss changing, demanding a response from Beth. Reluctantly he raised his head as they heard the voices of Casey and Mike approaching. His eyes were dark and heavy lidded as he looked at Beth, her lips swollen from his kiss. Almost against his will he raised a hand to touch her lips, a featherlike caress, then he turned and walked through the door, leaving an astonished Beth leaning against the wall.

Mike's astonished cry as he saw the kittens broke through her trance-like state. Shaking her head to clear it, she knelt and talked to the children about the care Gretel and the kittens would need in the future.

The kittens' arrival marked a change in Jenny. She took excellent care of Gretel and the kittens, carrying milk many times a day to them. She laughed easily; a smile seemingly fixed permanently on her face. She no longer hesitated to kiss or hug Murphy and Beth. Curling up in their laps at night, humming to herself while she played with her dolls. Her cheeks were rosy, and her eyes sparkled merrily, no longer the shy unhappy child who had arrived, she had blossomed into a loving, contented little girl. But she still refused to talk.

The kittens grew quickly, their eyes slowly opening after two weeks, their first tentative steps outside the box. Jenny delighted in their progress. Mike tried to help her name them. "Spot? Sally? Popeye? "his list seemed endless, but each time Jenny would shake her head.

As Beth finished the dishes one night, Murphy sat on the couch reading a bedtime story to Mike and Jenny. It was a Walt Disney Storybook of several of his popular stories, a gift from Miss Lucy to the children. This particular story was about Bambi. Murphy was sending the children into delightful giggles as he raised and lowered his voice to inflict the different animals with their own characteristics.

Beth listened to his voice, smiling herself at the sounds coming forth. Suddenly he stopped, "Jenny, what are you doing? Come back here and let me finish the story. Jenny?"

Jenny ran through the kitchen and out the door, an angry Mike and Murphy at her heels.

"Murphy! What's wrong?" Beth queried, following the trio out the door.

Murphy stopped for a minute to allow Beth to catch up, "I don't know, we were reading when suddenly Jenny grabs the book and takes off for the door."

"She's heading for Casey's, do you think she wants you to read to him, too?"

"I doubt it, look she's going into the shed. Now what the hell?"

"The kittens! I'll bet she's found names for the kittens in the book!" Beth exclaimed, as she grabbed his hand and hurried him along. As they opened the door, they found a sleepy Gretel yawning at Mike and Jenny. The kittens were crawling all over the floor. Jenny had opened the book and pointed to a picture.

Mike exclaimed, "She's got names for the kittens! Which one Jenny?" As Mike caught each tiny mewing bundle, Jenny pointed to a different picture in the book, the largest ginger was quickly named Bambi, the smallest, Thumper. The two calicos were dubbed Flower and Daisy. Once done, Jenny was very pleased with herself, she would hold one or the other as Mike called their names.

Murphy put his hand around Beth's shoulder, pulling her close to rest against him. She was all too aware of him, the hardness of his body, the scent of aftershave he wore. Steady, Beth said to herself, as she felt her knees weaken and her body lean towards his. Instead she turned and knelt down to hold one of the kittens in her arms, and as she turned Murphy's hand gently brushed her breast. A yearning filled her for more, but Murphy dropped his hand as if burned, Beth could feel his body stiffen and heard a quick intake of breath. Jenny took that moment to hand Murphy Bambi, smiling as she bestowed on him the honor of holding one of her kittens. Murphy's hand dwarfed the tiny fluff even as he managed to smile at Jenny and solemnly thank her. His eyes slowly rested on Beth, holding a tiny Thumper in her lap. The weight she had lost gave her face an almost ethereal quality, her eyes seemed to shine with a softness and warmth that filled her whole face. Her mouth was smiling as she watched the curious kittens and the children at play. A longing to hold her in his arms, to kiss her laughing lips was almost overwhelming.

She's getting under my skin, Murphy thought. She's so giving, so warm. God how I want her, need her! But I have to stay away, another voice warned. Keep her at arm's length just like all the others. But even as he thought the words, he discounted them knowing in his heart that here was a woman who was special, different from all the others. He knew that long after he sent her away, he would remember the feel of her lips against his, how her body seemed to mold to his as he held her, her laugh that would start with her eyes and end in the dimple in her chin, and her voice was so melodious even when she talked. Oh yes, thought Murphy, I'll remember, and wondered afresh why already he was dreading the day that she would leave.

The following morning found Beth doing her usual cleaning. Running the sweeper, she sang softly to herself, knowing that the noise of the sweeper drowned out her voice. It was a happy song of love and spring, her thoughts on Murphy and a fantasy ending to their marriage. She was dressed as usual in her jeans and a softly colored blouse tied around her midriff. Her hair was swept up into a hasty bun and already soft tendrils fell around her face. As Murphy came through the door, a grin spread across his features, thinking even at her worst, Beth was beautiful. His eyes lingering on the vulnerable neck beneath the wispy hair. He took a few steps and gently kissed her on her neck, feeling the pulse of her heart as he did.

Surprised, Beth whirled around, losing her balance and fell unceremoniously into Murphy's laughing arms. As he flicked the sweeper off with his foot, his arms tightened their grasp of Beth.

"Murphy," Beth began, "You scared me! That's not funny. Stop laughing at me! It's all your fault." She finished fighting the chuckle that arose in her throat and joined him. "What brings you up to the house at this time of day?"

Murphy dropped a kiss on her lips, before he answered her. "I'm delivering the mail," he grinned, "Is this how you always greet the mailman by falling into his arms? No wonder he was disappointed when I said I'd bring it in!"

He dropped the two letters from the pile in his hands before leafing through the rest. "You're a popular lady."

"Indeed, I am," she quipped, opening the first letter, already recognizing the handwriting of Uncle Henry. Reading quickly, she grinned, "Uncle Henry says you must not be beating me enough, I still sound too sassy in my letters."

"Mark that down, then, as of today, all beatings are doubled. Who's the other from?" he questioned quietly.

"It's got a Las Vegas postmark. Who do we know there?" she murmured as she slit open the envelope, "Johnny! the darling," she went on, unaware of the look of displeasure that had settled on his face on hearing his name. "He's coming to St. Louis and wants to know if we can get together. "She lifted glowing eyes to look at Murphy, "Can we? Maybe he could stay in the spare bedroom for a couple of days." her voice flattened as she noticed the anger in Murphy's face.

His whole body was tense as he glared at Beth. His words harsh and menacing as he grabbed her by the shoulders roughly, "You are my wife," he bit out, "and while my wife you will not entertain another man in my own home!"

"Murphy, you don't understand."

"I understand all too well. Write him, call him, but let him know he is not welcome," he growled, his fingers digging into her shoulders with the intensity of his fury.

"I will not," Beth retorted with equal anger. "This happens to be my house, too. And as it's half mine for the remainder of the year, I can choose who can stay as well as you can. Johnny is coming," she stated defiantly. Her hazel eyes almost emerald as she met his gaze, trying to free herself from the vice like grip on her shoulders.

"If you invite him into this house, then you will be responsible when I throw lover boy out!" he roared.

"If you think of Johnny as my lover boy then you're a fool, Murphy Whitaker! How can you think that we...that I ...You must have really gathered a high class of woman around you over the years."? Beth shouted back, sarcasm giving them a bitter sound, "If after all these weeks, you still see me as just like them, then it doesn't make any difference if Johnny comes. Because if he doesn't, you'll probably imagine me meeting him in some sleazy motel, now let go of me." She pulled her arms free, rubbing the shoulders where he had held her. Murphy stood glaring at her, his hands, hard fists at his side.

Beth continued, her voice shook with emotion and frustration, "Not once have I ever given you reason to mistrust me! But you do! Not once have I questioned your motives or your intentions, but you constantly see me as a conniving, scheming, two-timer." A sob came from deep within her, "Murphy I don't think I want to be friends any more. Friends," she said, "trust each other." As tears ran down her cheeks, she ran from the room and out the door. She almost collided with Jenny; her arms full of kittens.

"Let's go for a walk, love," Beth murmured, "Yes, we'll take them with us, but only two, okay?" She kept her head down, hoping Jenny would not notice her tears, her hand hastily wiping her eyes. She looked up for a glimpse of Mike and saw him walking with Casey. She hurried off across the field, Jenny running after her, clutching Bambi and Thumper in her arms.

Oh, Murphy, Beth thought, what am I to do now? How can I stay here, loving you but knowing you'll never return that love? Remembering Murphy's opinion of her brought fresh pain to her heart. She glanced down at the struggling Jenny, "Hop up on my back love, I'll give you a piggyback ride. I'll hold the kittens right here, okay?" Walking with the solemn Jenny calmed Beth but created new heartbreak at the thought of leaving them. She so loved the two children.

They soon approached the orchard. Late spring had brought the trees blossoming in tiny white and pink snow like flowers. The scent filled the air, as Beth looked down the rows and rows of heavily laden trees. Finding a grassy hollow, she gently let the little girl down and placed the kittens in her lap. She watched them stretch, walking slowly, tentatively on the grass. Bambi seemed to be stalking a cricket as he scampered about. Thumper tried to swat a piece of clover with its paw, their antics caused Beth to smile and Jenny to laugh. Beth leaned back in the grass, closing her eyes to the bright spring sun and the hopelessness of a future without Jenny, Mike and Murphy. She must have dazed as she woke to the urgent pulling of her arm by Jenny, the sun no longer bright but setting slowly over the distant hills.

Still half asleep she leaned on one arm, "What is it love?" she questioned. At Jenny's distressed face, she straightened and let Jenny lead her to a nearby tree. Thumper sat contently at the foot of the tree, but a plaintiff mew could be heard from higher up. Looking up, Beth saw a frightened kitten half-way up the tree.

"Oh Bambi!" Beth moaned, "Now how on earth did you manage to get way up there? It's alright Jenny," she assured the little girl, "I'll just climb up and get him, you stay put. Well, here goes."

Beth slowly climbed up the tree, grateful that the branches were close enough for her to pull herself up on. She glanced down and waved to Jenny, "It's all right, I'm almost there," she shouted. She went up two more limbs, and slowly stood up. Reaching around the tree, she carefully put her hand on the kitten. Being frightened though, Bambi had no intention of letting loose of his claws from the bark. "Let go, babe," Beth coaxed as she pulled gently forcing Bambi to release his hold. "There love, you're all right." she told the little kitten, "Now we just go down." Holding him gently with one hand and descending with the other was more difficult than Beth imagined. Her foot sought the lower branch as she held on to the one above her, the kitten moved, startling Beth, she slipped, her free arm hitting the limb as she fell, she rolled as she hit the grass and lay still. Her fingers loosening on the terrified kitten. Jenny ran to where Beth lay, shaking her arm, urging her as she had previously to wake up. She touched her hair, brushing it back from Beth's face, as she did, she saw the red stain covering her cheek. Jenny stared at the blood, her small face turning white. "No!" she screamed. "No...No!" She stood up, running back through the darkening twilight towards the farm.

After Beth had left, Murphy stayed in the living room, hearing her walk away with Jenny. He had slumped down into the chair, his eyes closed to shut out the memory of Beth's pale face, her eyes filled with tears. His fist hit the arm of the chair as he vented his anger at himself. You fool, he thought. Why did you let your jealousy loose on her! She's right you know, what has she ever done to cause you to mistrust her, nothing. Nothing but give herself to the kids and the house unselfishly since she got here, he moaned. He thought again of her happiness at hearing from Johnny. Again, Murphy felt the urge to punish the man who brought the smile to Beth's eyes. His thoughts went further as he imagined his Beth in Johnny's arms. "No!" Murphy groaned, his voice startling the silence that filled the room. Equally as startling was the realization to Murphy why he felt so intensely about Johnny. I love her, Murphy thought, My God, I love her! His mind churning, remembering how angry she had been, remembering too the last words she had spoken to him. "Friends trust each other!"

"Love means trust, too," he thought dejectedly, "I didn't show any, I don't deserve her trust." Resolutely he stood up and left the house. Each step convincing him that he had a difficult task ahead in proving to Beth he could trust, an even harder one convincing himself he was worthy of that trust.

It was a grim Murphy that worked the rest of the afternoon, plowing the fields all afternoon, feeding the livestock, and locking things up in the growing dusk, his mind rehearsing the words of apology for Beth. A distracted Murphy listened to the teasing banter between Casey and Mike as they brought the basket of fresh eggs up from the hen house. Together the three of them walked into the kitchen door, expecting to find a busy Beth and Jenny putting the last touches to their evening meal. No warm smells greeted them, and even worse no brown haired, slender Beth warmed the room. A cold feeling of dread clutched at his heart. "Beth," he said, "Beth?" raising his voice to be heard throughout the house.

Casey spoke from the doorway, "Her car's here, Mr. Murphy, maybe she went walking, she'll be here shortly."

Murphy remembered seeing her heading across the field after their angry exchange of words. But that was hours ago, she should be back by now, knowing that even if Beth were still angry, she would still have cooked supper, still have taken care of the children.

Casey was talking to Mike, "What say we cook supper for your Aunt Beth, Mike? Do you think she'd like that?"

"Do you know how to cook, Casey?" Mike asked innocently.

"Course I do," he mumbled. "Not like your Aunt Beth, but we won't starve!" He looked at the great shape that had not moved from the doorway, his sharp eyes noticing the lines of worry about Murphy's mouth.

"You all right, Murphy?" He asked softly. Disturbing the painful thoughts of where Beth might be, he shook his head slowly. Becoming slowly aware of the barking of Bingo near the back steps and the whining of Dusty, he opened the door to look out into the fields beyond the house. A movement caught his eye as a small shape stopped and then started moving again. As Murphy realized what the shape was, he was out the door and across the yard. A puzzled Casey and Mike following in his wake. Murphy hurdled the fence and reached Jenny's side before she could take another step. He held the sobbing, trembling figure close as she grasped his neck convulsively, long sobs shaking her entire body as her lungs tried painfully to draw the breath she needed to speak.

"Where's Beth, Jenny?" Murphy urgently asked. "Jenny, please--where is she?" Fear gripped his heart as he silently urged Jenny to answer.

Jenny drew a shaking breath, "Beth ...hurt ...blood."

"Where," Murphy pleaded, "My God, where Jenny?"

"Trees ... flowers ..." Jenny spoke in gasps.

"Jenny," Murphy whispered urgently "where were the flowers? By the creek?" Her small head shook.

Casey interrupted, "Were the flowers on the trees, Jenny?"

At her nod, "The orchards," Casey said. "The flowering trees have to be the fruit trees."

"Right," Murphy said. "Call Father Mac, have him meet me at the orchards, and call an ambulance. I'm heading across the fields, its quicker. Meet me with the truck." He touched the tears on Jenny's cheeks, "She'll be all right, thank you, Jenny," he kissed her forehead, "You're a brave little girl." Without another glance he headed off across the fields in the direction he had seen Jenny come. Running as he had many years ago playing football with the opposing defense at his heels, only this time the thought that he might not be in time quickened his long strides. It seemed an eternity as he vaulted fences and skirted irrigation ditches. The fields had never seemed so wide, as he ran, his breath uneven, his body unprepared for his marathon. "Oh God," he prayed, "Please, ... please let Beth be all right." His mind kept echoing her last words, "I don't want to be your friend." Murphy's face tightened, as grim lines told of his thoughts. Just let her be alright, give me one more chance! Just one. He saw the white topped trees now, even in the waning light the aroma of the trees together with the soft white petals was breathtakingly beautiful. Murphy saw no beauty; he saw only a place where Beth lay hurt. The small orchard suddenly loomed dark and menacing. Murphy started calling her name, his ears straining for a sound, any sound that could show him where she lay. He took tentative steps through the rows. His eyes alert for any movement. His ears heard the crickets of early spring, a few frogs, and a mewing that Murphy couldn't place. He ran his hand distractedly through his hair, when realization of the mewing stopped all motion. He walked quickly towards the sound, hoping as he walked that the kittens Jenny had held as she left with Beth had stayed. The sounds intensified as he hurried down the rows. His eyes searched thoroughly when he saw a slight movement from the corner of his eye.

"Beth?" he asked, his voice shaking.

"Beth!" he shouted when there was still no answer. He knelt beside the still form, two kittens mewing helplessly from her arms. He cursed beneath his breath at having no light to search for her injuries. His hands felt her arms. They felt cool beneath his touch. He lowered his head to listen for her heartbeat, to hear the breath as it entered her body. Impatiently his hand sought her pulse beneath her right ear on the slender neck. Murphy held his own breath, afraid for the silence he might hear. A tiny threadlike beat could be felt, so faint as to be almost nonexistent. A ragged sigh escaped his lips, relief at finding her alive, and a determination to keep her that way. Gently he felt her arms, noting what was probably a break in her left forearm. He felt down her legs; her right was twisted under her body.

He heard his name, and yelled in return, urging Father Mac to hurry. Father Mac had a flashlight and its bright light showed the pallor of Beth's skin, carefully Murphy felt her head. His hand stopped when he felt a bump, removing his hand as he felt the warm sticky blood.

"Oh my God!" Murphy muttered, his face paling beneath his tan. He raised anguished eyes to Father Mac, beseeching his help, anyone's help to save his wife. Murphy removed his shirt, tearing the sleeve to wrap around her head, hoping to slow the flow of life-giving warmth from her body. The rest he laid over her to ward off the effects of shock. Suddenly the darkness was filled with the lights of the truck, bearing down on the orchard. Faintly they could hear the siren of the ambulance as it turned, following the truck's lights.

Casey, Mike and Jenny were climbing out of the truck, running to where they knelt.

Murphy handed the kittens gently to Jenny, his face never leaving Beth. His face flinching as they lifted her body to the stretcher revealing the dark circle of red earth beneath her head.

A tiny hand slipped into his, bringing him back to the reality of Mike and Jenny. He squeezed the hand, then glanced at Casey, his eyes asking as no words formed on his dry lips.

"I'll take care of them, Mr. Murphy," Casey said quietly, "Don't give them another thought, I'll see to everything."

Father Mac laid a comforting hand on Murphy's shoulder, "I'll follow you in your truck. You go ahead and ride with Beth in the ambulance. Have faith, my son."

Murphy nodded numbly, grateful for their understanding. He followed the stretcher into the ambulance. His eyes never wavering from the pale face on the bed. His hand moved unthinkingly to brush her hair from her check, his touch light as a feather. She felt cold, so cold, almost as if... his hands clenched, his brow broke out in perspiration with the thought that he might never be able to tell her of his love, hear her laughter, feel the touch of her skin, see her eyes sparkling in anger, warm in her joy. His eyes swam at the frustration of not being able to do anything. God, he thought, Oh God! Let her live! His cry of anguish, taking her pain as his, willing his strength to her.

The ride seemed interminable as cars and lights whizzed by. The Mississippi dark, murky, winding, the barges only twinkling lights in the distance, the cliffs, majestic against a sky filled with stars, the trees filled with the promise of new life. Past the tall silos of grain, the silent elevators, over the cobblestone streets, and up the countless hills that Alton consisted of. Finally, entering the tree lined sanctuary that surrounded the hospital.

Murphy dismounted following close behind Beth as they entered the large double doors of the Alton

Memorial Hospital Emergency Room. Nurses hurried forward, taking her pulse while they wheeled her into a small brightly lit cubicle. Deft, practiced hands cut her soiled clothing, changing the wounds as they worked. Still she did not move. Blood tests were quickly taken and sent to the laboratory for immediate match and cross-matching.

A hand touched Murphy's arms, a white uniformed nurse stood at his side, "Sir, we need some information." He nodded. "Are you her husband?" she continued.

"Yes," Murphy's voice was little more than a moan.

"Her name?"

"Elizabeth Anne Whitaker."

"Her age?"

"Twenty-Four."

Her voice went on, she asked, Murphy answering in monocyclic replies, but his eyes remained on Beth. Presently, they were joined by the doctor, the nurse pulled a curtain, blocking Murphy's entrance to the room. An apologetic smile, asking him to please wait outside, the doctor would see him in a few minutes.

Murphy stared at the entrance desk, he paced the hall, he willed for someone to come from behind that curtain to tell him she would be all right.

He looked up as Father Mac arrived, wordlessly handing Murphy another shirt. He looked down, only then remembering he had used his on Beth. As he slipped it on, he mumbled to Father Mac, "They're examining her now."

The wait seemed endless as he watched nurses enter, then leave, listening to the muted words behind the screen. Finally, the doctor emerged, a slight man of medium height, his hair thinning slightly, wire rimmed glasses resting on a straight nose. He shook Murphy's hand introducing himself as Dr. Townsend, he wasted no time in briefing Murphy on his wife's condition. "She has a broken arm, a fractured femur, some internal bleeding, and a concussion causing swelling and pressure to her brain. We need to operate immediately, to repair the damage internally and to relieve the pressure on her brain. Unfortunately," he went on, "it seems your wife is a rare blood type. I'm checking the other hospitals now to locate enough to enable us to begin as quickly as possible."

"Can I...We" (as he saw Father Mac nod), "donate blood?" Murphy asked swiftly.

"Of course, but the chance of you being the right type is very slim. Now, if you'll excuse me," he walked away, turning as he reached the door, "She shows scars from another accident; it's a possibility she may have received transfusions then, you might try locating someone who might have donated at that hospital."

Murphy watched as they wheeled Beth from the room, he started to follow, only to be stopped by the nurse. "Sorry, sir, we're preparing your wife for surgery and you are not permitted in the room."

"Can I...see her before she goes up?"

"Yes, but only for a few seconds. I'll send someone when we're ready."

As they disappeared down the hall, Murphy walked decisively to the phones located at the reception area. He received change from the information desk and to the amazement of Father Mac who hoovered nearby, proceeded to place a person to person call to a Henry Daniels in San Diego, California.

"Daniels?" his voice broke into the silence of the area, "Murphy here. Beth's had an accident. She needs blood. Did she receive any in that night club accident two years ago?"

"From whom, did they tell you the name of the donor?"

"Who did you say?" his voice expressionless as he listened to Daniels repeating the name of Johnny Duncan. "Daniels, do you have his number?"

"1-634-976-4492."

"Thanks, we'll be in touch and let you know how she is." He hung up and dialed the number Henry Daniels had given him, his hand holding the phone so tightly his knuckles showed white.

"Hello... I need to reach Johnny Duncan...it's an emergency--tell him ... tell him it concerns Beth Whitaker ... Yes, I'll hold."

Seconds ticked by, seeming like hours, as he held the phone waiting. "Hello, Duncan? This is Murphy Whitaker ... that's right, Beth's husband ...There's been an accident, she needs blood ...Dammit man, of course it's serious, do you think I'd be calling you if it weren't!" Murphy erupted into the phone. " ...Good, we'll have someone waiting on the next flight in from Las Vegas to pick you up...Duncan, thanks," he murmured, the tight control he had managed all evening seeming to crumple as he buried his head in his hands.

CHAPTER 11

Murphy stood grimly at the entrance, waiting impatiently for the arrival of Father Mac with Johnny Duncan. His eyes watched each stranger approach, but his mind constantly strayed to the stolen minutes with Beth before she was taken up to the operating room. Still unconscious, he had held her hand, kissing her palm, each finger, his voice was low, gentle as he told her how much he loved her and how she had to get better for him, the kids. As his allotted time sped by, he gently kissed her lips, lingering on their softness, drawing strength from their sweetness. As he raised his head, he kissed each eyelid and whispered one last final phrase, "I trust you friend," as they silently wheeled her away.

He caught the approach of Father Mac and someone else...Johnny Duncan. As they walked up the sidewalk, Murphy had time to study the man who could...would save his wife's life. He wasn't a tall man, probably no taller than Beth herself. Dressed in the clothes he had been wearing when he received his call, black slacks with a shirt of silver unbuttoned to his waist. Several silver chains hung about his neck. His light brown hair feathered back, showing a round, high forehead. Dark sunglasses covered his eyes and shielded the prominent cheek bones and a long, aristocratic nose. His mouth was stretched into a grim line as he talked to Father

Mac. Johnny looked up as they entered the entrance to the huge man standing directly in front of him. He recognized him from the description Beth had written. Except she had spoken of the warmth from his eyes and the laughter.   Today there was no laughter, and no warmth. Johnny raised his hand; Murphy grasped his in a vice like grip.

"They're waiting. This way." He led the two to the laboratory where lab technicians waited to begin the preparation for the transfusion.

It was a strange group of people who waited for news of Beth in the reception room outside the operating theatre, one priest, one musician, one small leprechaun, and a man whose presence dwarfed the entire room, almost as much as his height dwarfed the others in size. Each man was lost in their own thoughts. Murphy's hands rested in the windowsill of the large picturesque room. He stared stonily out the window, unseeing of the idyllic setting of the hospital.

Nestled among acres of huge oaks and maples, the hospital was in the middle of the city of Alton. But so carefully had it been planned that even looking out the windows from the highest floor, all one saw were quiet, beautiful trees. The only sounds were those of the birds that abounded the woods and bushes. A trickling brook ran amongst the acres, a clear, serene babble that gave water and life to the surrounding hills. A myriad of flowers had been planted from the paths and walkways giving the appearance of walking through a garden of a palatial home instead of the lawn of a huge city hospital.

Murphy saw nothing of the beauty, but his soul sensed the tranquility of his surroundings. He sighed, wondering for the thousandth time how much longer

Beth would be in the operating room. An old adage came to mind, 'No news is good news,' trying to draw comfort from the phrase as he looked again at his watch. His hand went abstractly through his hair, his face showing the strain and tiredness of the past hours through the long night.

Oh Beth, he thought, you've got to make it! Murphy pictured them on a picnic after she was well. He could see the laughter in her eyes as Mike and Jenny scrambled over the rocks and driftwood littering the Mississippi shore. He also hoped to see love in their hazel depths, a love born of trust and friendship. He could see her smiling up at himself, the dimple showing in her cheek. He could feel her lips, moving sensuously beneath his. The touch of her hands against his chest. He closed his eyes to shut out the memories.

Footsteps sounded in the hall, all eyes watched as the doctor arrived, still dressed in his blue surgical gown. He sought the face of Murphy as he entered the room.

"Beth... is she, all right?" Murphy's voice broke the silence.

"We've completed surgery, both the internal injuries and relieved the pressure off the brain. Her arm has been set as well as her leg, if that's what you mean by all right." He smiled at the strained, pale face of the man before him, "She'll make it, young man. You've a strong, brave wife. She's in intensive care right now, but you can go in as soon as she's been set up."

Murphy gave the doctor a hearty shake, barely able to murmur his thanks. He turned to face to the trio of anxious faces still in the room. "She'll be okay, she's going to be all right," he assured them, unashamed of the tears that filled his eyes.

Beth tried to open her eyes, they seemed so heavy, she turned her head, only to have a sharp pain still her movement. A groan escaped her lips, she heard a murmur of voices, was that Murphy's voice she heard? He sounded strange. She lifted her hand to rub her eyes, only to find she couldn't move it.

"Beth, darling," surely that couldn't be Murphy's voice, so gentle and loving. I must be dreaming, she thought, anxious for the pleasant dream to continue.

"Beth, don't move. You fell from the tree, remember? Don't try and speak just squeeze my hand...That's my girl... "He paused looking at the bandaged head of the frail delicate woman in the bed. Her skin so clear as to appear translucent, dark shadows surrounded her eyes as the discoloration of the bruise colored her temple. "You're in the hospital...You had a nasty bump on your temple. They had to relieve the pressure; your arm is broken as well as your leg. You probably ache from head to toe, but the doctor assures us you'll be fine and up in a few weeks."

Beth licked dry, cracked lips. "Jenny?"

"... is fine and so is Mike. Jenny ran and told us you were hurt. She talked Beth...the silence is broken. She's been very worried about you, but she's jabbering away now."

Beth smiled, " ... so glad... " she murmured, finding it very difficult to concentrate as she drifted back to sleep, barely catching Murphy's last words "... love you ... "

The next time she woke up, her eyes managed to open completely. Beth looked around the room, a dark shape slumped in the chair by the bed. There lay Murphy, a dark stubble of growth grew on his chin, his clothes crumpled. Beth sighed, he looked so vulnerable sleeping in that chair. His long lashes a shadow on his cheek, how she longed to touch his face. Her forehead creased in thought trying to remember something he had said earlier, it seemed so important, she must remember, her free hand moved to touch her head, the slight movement waking the slumbering giant.

"Beth?" he said sleepily, "How are you feeling?" And then Beth saw Johnny sitting in a chair by the window.

"Johnny!" Beth exclaimed, "What are you doing here?"

"Your husband sent for me."

Beth turned confused eyes to Murphy, finding it very important that he tell her why when the last time they had talked he had been so adamant in his opinion of Johnny. "Murphy, why did you send for Johnny?" Her eyes locking his gaze, surprised at the wave of emotion she saw struggling in their depths.

Johnny broke into their silence, "You needed a transfusion, love. Since our type matched, Murphy cut through a lot of red tape by just carting me over here. He's not a man to be argued with, is he love?"

Murphy gave a rueful smile, "Beth finds no trouble arguing with me, Johnny." He stood up, towering over the bed. "I think I'll go home and get cleaned up," he told Beth, "I'll be back later tonight, okay?"

"Only if you'll get some sleep first?" she told him, then smiled, "Unless you want to end up a patient here, too? Are there family rates?" As she smiled, Murphy caught his breath--how achingly dear her smile was, he

145

kissed her, a featherlike caress, before he walked to the door, only pausing long enough to issue a firm warning to Johnny not to tire her before he was gone.

Johnny gave an impish grin to Beth after he had gone, "Good Lord," he said, "That's a hell-of-a man to be in love with!"

Beth laughed softly, "He does take your breath away, doesn't he?" She grew serious, "Do you like him?"

"I don't know yet," Johnny said slowly, "I really haven't decided. But one thing is in his favor," he paused, "...He loves you with an intensity I'd be hard pressed to find fault with."

Beth was astonished, "Whatever makes you say that?"

"Beth, you know that anytime you needed me, I would have come. Well, your Murphy didn't stop to ask me, he told me 'Be here!' I heard his voice, I may have been two thousand miles away, but I knew God help me, if I wasn't in time. When I arrived, he didn't speak two words to me, he was almost demented with worry. Then when they came to us after the operation, Beth, there's no words to express the relief I saw in his face. Then there's the fact that he hasn't left your side since he found you in the orchard from what I've gathered from Father Mac, not to eat, or sleep. I think he has half the nurses in this hospital waiting on his every word, and each word has been to ask how you were."

"Oh," she said, feeling very warm as she blushed.

"Oh? Is that all" Johnny teased taking a shrewd look at the girl in the bed. "Tell me, love, how goes the marriage...He loves you...You love him, but all's not right is it?"

A small shake of her head was all Beth could do as memory of their last argument played before her eyes.

"Talk to me, then, let me see if I can help," he asked.

"You can't, Johnny, I wish you could, but he doesn't trust me, you see. And trust is such an important part of friendship and marriage." her voice faded.

"Go to sleep, Beth" he said soothingly. "We'll talk when you've rested, I for one have no intention of making your husband mad at me! Sleep, love ... "He watched Beth drift back into a peaceful slumber wondering what could be behind the unhappiness he saw in her eyes and determined to solve it.

Johnny was waiting for Murphy when he returned that night outside Beth's room. His expression grim as he faced the concern in Murphy's eyes.

"Beth? Is she all right?" he began.

Johnny interrupted, "No, she's not. But it's nothing these doctors can fix. I think it's time we had a little talk."

As Murphy ignored him, Johnny leaned across, "Beth's asleep, if you care about her at all, I think you had better decide to have our talk."

Murphy turned eyes of flint to stare at Johnny, anger emanating from his body.

Johnny took a deep, steadying breath, "You can cream me probably with one hand behind your back. You're twice the size I am. But the point remains that I do care about your wife and I don't want to see her unhappy." he paused. "So, what's it to be Murphy, do we talk, or do you fight?"

Murphy gave a brief angry jerk of his head, indicating to Johnny toward the reception room down the hall. Murphy shut the door as they entered, "Talk, Duncan, you've got five minutes." The words were clipped revealing a slim control over his anger.

"Does Beth know you love her?" Johnny demanded.

"What business is that of yours?"

"Every right," Johnny retorted, "I love her too, and I'm not going to stand by while some ex-jock makes her life miserable. Besides which... "

"Besides which nothing," Murphy gritted, his fists tightly clenched around Johnny's shirt. "She's my wife, and you or anybody else is going to come between us... "

"...she's my sister." Johnny finished.

Murphy's hands released him as if burnt, a stunned look appearing on his face, "Your sister?!" he asked incredulously, "How, Why?"

A gentler Johnny motioned for him to sit. "You didn't know? No, of course not ... If you did, you wouldn't have regarded me as competition. Let me explain, I gather Beth told you about her parents, the ones that died when she was about sixteen, right?" At his nod, "Right, well those were Beth's parents, her adoptive parents. Our own parents were killed shortly after she was born, I'm fourteen years older than her, I remember them. When they were killed, we went to a home. I remember what a beautiful baby Beth was, everybody was crazy about her. Babies are easy to place in a home, but nobody wants a 14-year-old kid. I figured for Beth to have any sort of a normal life. I'd have to disappear. I had it all carefully planned, I even left a note, so they'd know to let her go to a good home, but on paper we were still a twosome. I hitchhiked around, got odd jobs. But I kept track of Beth. After about a year, I called Henry Daniels. He was our parents' lawyer and I knew I could trust him not to turn me in. I explained about Beth, needing a home and all and he agreed to help on the condition that I come and live with him, only until I finished school. I'd been sleeping in an old deserted building; believe me it was no hardship to accept besides which at Henry's I could play his piano. Beth, in due course, was adopted by the Riley's, a super couple, I used to mow their lawn just to catch a glimpse of her. I won a music scholarship from school, and never looked back except to keep in touch with Henry about Beth. She grew up, I don't know it they planned on telling Beth she was adopted or not, they died, and Beth didn't know. Again, our good friend Henry stepped in, this time offering his home to Beth. I was in a position to help her now, but I was a stranger. She didn't even know she had a brother! She'd had some pretty rough shocks; I wasn't adding to them. She finished school, then college and she started singing, I used to sit at the back of the joint she played at and just listen. It was a joy just to hear. When she graduated from college, I arranged to meet her and team up singing with me. The rest you probably know."

"Not quite," Murphy mentioned, "when did she realize you were her brother?"

"You know about the fire?"

"Yes, Beth told me."

"Did you know she saved my life? She dragged me out of the club, at the expense of her own injuries. I'd collapsed, but she wouldn't leave me. Later, when she needed transfusions, I was the perfect choice. Beth's a smart cookie. I think down deep she'd always felt a kinship with me, but the blood kind of clinched things in her mind. She asked and Henry and I told her. She's quite a girl."

"I'll agree to that," Murphy said quietly, he stuck out his hand, "Welcome to the family, Johnny, I apologize for my rudeness. I'd like to be friends with my brother-in-law."

Johnny clasped the hand, wincing at Murphy's firm clasp. "The first thing we do, 'friend' is to remember I earn my living by these hands! Any more handshakes like those and I'll file for disability!"

Murphy laughed, "You're on. By the way Casey's outside in the truck. We'd like you to stay at the house if you can now and whenever you're playing in St. Louis. Beth...we'd both like it very much if you could see your way clear to stay with us. We do have a piano if that's any consolation?"

Johnny smiled, "You just talked yourself into a visitor, Murphy. Remember, when I wear out my welcome, that you did ask."

They walked back to Beth's room, at her door Johnny turned to ask him and grinned, "By the way, tell Beth 'I do' when she wakes up. She'll know what you're talking about." He went whistling softly down the hall.

Murphy smiled and entered Beth's room, surprised to find her sitting up, her hair combed to hide the bandage, and wearing a pale lime nightgown.

"Sick people aren't supposed to look incredibly beautiful." Murphy said.

"I'm not sick, I'm injured," Beth retorted, a blush covering her pale face.

"That explains it then," Murphy chuckled, "Mrs. Whitaker, you look beautiful."

150

"Thank you, Mr. Whitaker. It's amazing what a girl has to do to be told she's beautiful around here. By the way, the flowers are gorgeous! Thank you, but I'm a little confused by the message. Perhaps you'd care to explain?" She lifted a small white card from her hand. "It says 'To my wife and dearest friend, with trust, Murphy.'"

Murphy seated himself on the bed, "Johnny said to give you a message. He said to tell you 'I do', that you'd understand."

"I'm glad, when did you talk to Johnny?" a tiny frown beginning to form, she lowered her eyes afraid to hear his answer.

"Beth, darling," Murphy began, "Look at me. Please," as he met her sad tortured glance, he smiled, "I sent the flowers before I left the hospital this afternoon, I talked to Johnny just a few minutes ago."

"You...You didn't know he was my brother when you wrote the note?" Beth asked insistently.

"No, love. I had decided before your accident that I loved you and with that love was trust. I was waiting to tell you, but you never came back."

"You love me?" her voice faltered, unable to believe her ears.

"I love you so much that the fear of losing you to death or anyone else terrifies me. I know I've been a swine. I take you for granted, I yell at you, if you'll just give me a chance, I'll be patient, I won't pressure you, I promise."

"Oh, Murphy," Beth cried happily, "I love you...I have from the very start!"

Her words were lost at the touch of his lips on hers, his mouth an ecstasy of sensual pleasure. He kissed her eyes, her nose, gently finding her lips yet again. "I almost lost you," Murphy murmured, his voice filled with emotion, "God, I love you, Beth."

"And I, dear husband, love you with all my heart." She sighed, "It looks like it'll be awhile before I can show you how much." She looked at her casts wryly, "They're better than a chastity belt!"

"I'll wait," Murphy replied, "besides which, we'll have time to see to rather pressing matters first." Beth's astonished look had him kissing her again, quickly as he held her chin in his hand. "Beth, my love, will you do me the great honor of becoming my wife?"

"But Murphy, we were married months ago before we ever came here..."

"You once told me that you would never feel really married unless you were married by a priest. I want you to feel really married, Beth, to me, and to have no doubts that you're well and truly married, for always. I ask again, will you marry me?"

"Oh, Murphy," Beth's eyes filled with tears, "I'd like more than anything else in the world to be well and truly married to you...forever."

Not trusting himself to kiss her once again, he slowly pressed each finger to his lips. "So be it, my love. Your casts are removed in six weeks. Does a wedding in late June meet with your approval?"

Her eyes glowed as she happily agreed. "If we can, would you like to be married at St. Mary's by Father Mac?"

"Oh, Murphy, can we?"

"We, dear heart, can do anything we damn well please! I only have one request. I want to see you wearing the same dress as before. I don't remember what it even looks like, but I'm still haunted by the vision of you on that day. I think I probably lost my heart to you then and there, but being pretty dense, it took a while to sink in. Even longer to accept that I could not live without you!"

"And then there was Johnny," Beth murmured. "You were so angry!"

"I heard you tell him you loved him on the phone. I could have broken his neck. I was just beginning to trust you and convince myself you were different, only to be proven wrong. If you only knew the agony, I went through thinking about someone else holding you in their arms!"

"Probably very similar to what I felt when Celia told me you'd been engaged to Mike and Jenny's mother," Beth added, reluctant to spoil their happiness but wanting reassurance about the only cloud she felt.

"Aha! So that has been bothering you. I rather hoped you'd be jealous. But you were so cool and calm, I guess I'd better explain."

"Only if you want to. I'll be honest, I'm dying to know but you don't have to talk about it, if you don't want to. "

"Hush, love, I don't mind. In fact, I rather think I'd better. I want no secrets clouding our future." He took a deep breath, still holding her hand, his thumb caressing her pulse as he talked. "You know that I played football?"

"Los Angeles Trojans, number forty-two, wide receiver and outstanding rookie for your first year. I hear you also managed to rush for over 1000 yards every season you played." Beth quoted, then grinned,

"Johnny's a great football fan. He told me all your statistics this afternoon."

"I like your brother more all the time," he leaned to kiss her upturned lips. "Now don't distract me or I'll make you wait until tomorrow to hear all about Joanna!"

"Yes sir," Beth grinned impishly.

"Yes, well, while playing I met a lot of women. They had different faces, but they were all the same. They wanted to be seen with me, my money, and the spotlight. I got pretty cynical during those years and I was lonely. Marshall wrote, of course, but I still felt alone. At a party I met Celia and her sister, Joanna. Both lovely to look at but as different as you can imagine inside. Celia, I shunned, but Joanna was a nice change. She laughed a lot and didn't tell me things I knew weren't true. She told me that night that she liked me and wondered if we could be friends. We saw a lot of each other, but we were just friends. We did a lot of talking, listening. How can I explain, she was my friend because she liked me, not because she could use me? She met Marshall one weekend when he came to visit. For Jo it was love at first sight. She and Marshall spent his entire stay together. But he left. They had an argument over one of those gossip columns linking her with me. She found out she was pregnant and too proud to tell Marshall. I asked her to marry me only to give the Whitaker name to my brother's child and because she was a very good friend." He looked lovingly and longingly into Beth's eyes. "I never told her I loved her. I've never been able to say that to anyone, until now."

Beth smiled, her eyes mirroring her love, "It's all right, Murphy. I love you too, remember? Now go on with your story, please?"

He grinned, kissed her nose impudently and continued. "When Marshall heard about the engagement, he was furious, called me every name in the book and then flew over. I was on the way to the airport to pick him up when I had the accident. I was out for a while, concussion, stitches, that type of thing. When I came to, Marshall knew about the baby and why I was engaged to Jo. He wanted to marry her, and I gave my blessings. Unfortunately, papers being what they were drew their own conclusions. They had a heyday! My injuries put me out for the football season, gave me time to think about me. Did I really want to spend the next couple of years being chased by 200-pound defensive tackles?

"I talked with Marsh. He needed a decent job, what with a family to support and all and I wanted to be my own boss. We went together and started our own computer company, very small at first. That first year I worked in this little building 24 hours a day, designing and then training the people to make it, my way. Marshall sold them. He was all over this country. Sometimes he'd take Jo with him, that's how they both came to be flying when they crashed."

"That first year we managed to break even, barely. After that we never looked back. You may not know, Mrs. Whitaker, but you are married to a very wealthy man."

"It really doesn't matter, you know." Beth said softly.

"I know, love, that's what makes it so incredible. All those years, all that money! And no one I wanted to spend it on. I finally find one I'd like to buy the world for, and I have to live on what the farm makes!"

155

Beth's laughter echoed the room, "Well, I could use a new coffee pot!" She grew thoughtful, "Murphy, when we first met, you said you hadn't seen Mike or Jenny before. Didn't you go to their house? You worked together!"

"No, every time I saw them the gossip would start all over again. I stayed away, talked to them by phone. I did live a hermit's existence. Diamond Enterprises took all my time."

"You're the owner of The Diamond Company?"

"That's right. All Whitaker men have names that begin with an 'M'. Put the M over the W and you have two diamonds, our trademark."

"I'm suitably impressed, dear, but with Marshall gone and you here, who's running your business?"

"Our business, love, and as a matter of fact, I have, by phone. That's why I spend so many hours in the den, or at least I used to. You have made me neglect the business shamefully and I think you should be duly punished." He tried to look very severe, but his eyes shone spoiling the effect.

"Oh, dear," Beth giggled, "I'm terrified. What is to be my dire fate, kind sir?"

"A life sentence, I'm afraid, married to me." He pulled her into his arms and kissed her, a long sensuous kiss filled with promise for their future.

"Mr. Whitaker!" A stern voice spoke from the door. "Visiting hours have been over for half an hour. Your wife needs her rest," the nurse informed him.

"I'll go quietly, Ma'am," Murphy mocked. "Sleep well, love, see you in the morning." He delivered a brief kiss to Beth and walked to the door. Beth smiled dreamily and settled back in her bed.

CHAPTER 12

"Murphy, we will never be able to get all of these into the station wagon!" Beth moaned, as she looked around the room at the flowers that littered every available shelf and corner of the hospital room.

"Let that be a lesson to you, then. Don't have so many friends who care!" He grinned. "We could leave them you know. They can deliver them to all the people on this floor."

"What a good idea! But first I need all the cards so I can send thank you's." She hobbled over to the first only to be caught by two large hands and deposited gently in the waiting wheelchair.

"I'll collect the cards," Murphy declared firmly. "Your job is to sit and get better VERY quickly."

"I know, but I'm so bored by just sitting. I've missed Jenny and Mike dreadfully and I feel guilty about not being able to take care of them. But most of all, I don't want to wait another month to get married!"

Murphy chuckled wryly as he carried her case under one arm and whirled her out the door. "Not as much as I do, believe me!"

Beth was being discharged from the hospital. Her arm was still in a cast and her leg now sported a walking cast. She was going home. Her smile was radiant as she thanked the nurses. Once outside, she was carefully seated in the car. Murphy driving slowly down the exit.

"It feels so good to be going home! Are you sure Maria will be able to handle coming over every day to help without interfering with her own family?"

"Luke and Maria assured me they could manage. Maria wanted a job. This is one she can do close to home and bring her own kids with her. She'll make some money. We'll get some much-needed help for you. What is there to worry about?"

"I don't know," Beth chewed on her bottom lip. "It will just feel strange having someone else doing what I used to do. Who knows, you might like her cooking better than mine, and I'd be out of a job!"

"No way," Murphy declared. "The job you fill as my wife cannot be touched by anybody else. Not that anybody else wants to, but all the same ..."

"I love you, Murphy," Beth spoke, relieved that he was as sensitive to her thoughts to try and dispel her uneasiness. Changing the subject, "When is Johnny due back? Isn't his St. Louis debut pretty soon?"

"Hmmmm ...pretty soon. He'll let us know for sure. Settle back and rest now, I'll wake you when we hit the lane. You know that Mike and Jenny aren't going to give you a minute to yourself for a while, so put your head on my shoulder and sleep. Besides, it gives me a good excuse to hold you in my arms again." He kissed her hair as she snuggled down against him. All uneasiness disappeared as she gave a contented sigh and promptly slept. When they reached the lane, he gently kissed her, whispering as he did, "We're home, love."

Beth opened her eyes, looking with longing at the white fences, the hills of growing grain, and the comfortable old farmhouse that was their home.

"Murphy, can we still live here, even after the year is up?"

"We can, and we will. I love this farm too, Beth. There is no reason I can't make my base of operations here as somewhere else."

"Everything seems so quiet," Beth said, looking for signs of the children and Casey. "Where are they?"

"Let's go in and I'll look for them," Murphy said, picking her up easily in his strong arms. "Here I thought you'd want to be alone with me!"

"Well, I do," Beth giggled, "It's just that these two casts put a damper on things."

He opened the door with his hand and turned Beth into the living room as a crowd of people shouted, "Welcome Home, Beth!" Tears filled her eyes as she saw the room full of her friends. Casey held Mike and Jenny back as Murphy lowered her into the chair. Then they smothered her with hugs and kisses, telling her without words how much they had missed her. "I love you," she whispered at the two tiny heads at her knees. She looked around, there was Miss Lucy, standing very straight between Jim and Cindy Campbell, Maria and Luke Brown with Jason, Brian and Jill, their children, Father Mac was talking to Johnny and..." Uncle Henry!" Beth exclaimed, as she saw his familiar smile.

"Now you didn't really think I'd let you come home from the hospital and not be here to welcome you?" he asked her.

"It's so good to have you here, Uncle Henry!"

"From what you've gone through these last weeks, I figured I might be called to keep you out of trouble?" he chuckled, throwing a shrewd glance at Murphy, who had not taken his eyes from Beth since they came in. "Tell me, Murphy, is she more trouble than she's worth?"

"Not on your life, Daniels! And you know it!" Murphy chuckled, "I always said I trusted your judgment. I think I'll be forever in your debt for introducing me to Beth."

"Things working out to your satisfaction, then, eh?" he winked at the happy couple.

"Oh, Uncle Henry, Murphy and I are going to be married at the end of June in St. Mary's! Will you ...would you do us the honor of giving me away?" Beth smiled, her dimple showing.

"It would be my pleasure." he assured them; his eyes suddenly misty.

"Break it up, Henry. You can't go hogging the guest of honor all to yourself. Let the rest of us talk to her, too!" Johnny interrupted, bending low to kiss her cheek.

"How long are you going to be here, Johnny?" Beth asked.

"Well, I have a St. Louis engagement for the next three weeks and then I've got a special, once in a lifetime chance..." he grinned as he watched Beth's face fall "...to play the Ave Maria at my sister's wedding!"

"You brute! How could you do that to me!" Beth scolded, but her heart wasn't in it, and she gave up and grinned like everyone else. "Have you asked him yet?" she winked at Murphy.

He winked back and turned to Casey who was standing quietly behind Beth's chair. "This may sound very strange to you Casey, Beth and I are married, but it was a justice of the peace. We'd like to get remarried in the church. I need a best man...without my brother, you're the closest to family I've got. Beth thinks of you

160

as our lucky leprechaun. Would you be my best man, Casey?"

"Oh, please?" Beth reached up and touched his gnarled cheek, "it would mean so much to both of us. You're part of our family."

"I'd be right honored, Miss Beth." he sniffed, his eyes unusually bright. "Mr. Murphy, I'd best see about the cake and all." He bent to plant a hasty kiss on Beth's cheek before he scurried into the kitchen.

Murphy smiled at Beth, "Your turn, love."

"Mike, would you ask Miss Lucy to come here for a minute?" As she approached, Beth held out her hand, "Thanks for corning, Miss Lucy," she began.

"You should be," the elegant figure assured her, "instead of getting yourself all banged up, worrying us all, a simple invitation to come visit would have been much simpler." She smiled, "It's good to have you back. I've missed our visits."

"Me, too, I so enjoyed them. I was wondering if you would do a favor for me," she paused, "Murphy and I are getting married with the church's blessing. Father Mac is going to do our wedding and we have everything we need except," she smiled, "that I need a bridesmaid. Miss Lucy, would you consent to be my Maid of Honor? I think of you as a very dear friend. Would you, please?"

Quite taken back at the request, the aristocratic face paled, "I thought you were going to ask me for something old," she said, "Are you quite sure, Beth. Don't you want someone young?"

"Miss Lucy, at my wedding or any wedding, the people surrounding the bride and groom should be their family and closest friends. You are my dear friend. I

161

don't know of anyone I'd rather have," Beth said, her sincerity unquestionable.

"I'd love too," Miss Lucy told her, "and bless you for making an old lady happy." She sniffed, "Would you like to make me happier?"

"Sure, what do you want us to do?" Beth asked.

"Sing for us, Beth. I've missed listening to my favorite songbird."

"I will, but first we need to talk to two more very special people." She caught Murphy's hand and he knelt, drawing Mike and Jenny to their sides.

Murphy looked from Beth's shining eyes to the large expectant ones of the children. "Jenny, would you be our flower girl and Mike, would you be our ring bearer? You're a very special part of our family, too, you know!" He grinned at the children's' astonishment. It quickly turned to joy as they shouted in unison, "Would we!" and started kissing and hugging Beth and Murphy.

"Hey, you guys," Johnny shouted, "How about helping me play the piano?"

"Sure, Uncle Johnny!" and they scrambled across the floor to sit beside him. He started playing all their favorites, the children singing along. Their merriment was cut short by a sarcastic voice from the front door.

"How charming!" A furious Celia walked in dressed in a red jumpsuit. "I knocked, but over the racket, no one answered. I was left standing for ages!"

"If it isn't the wicked witch of the west," Murphy drawled. "To what do we owe this pleasure?"

Celia chose to ignore him and concentrated on the immobile figure seated beside him. "And what have you here? Murphy's handiwork, no doubt. Such a pity, but now you won't be able to take care of the kids." She

162

smiled, "That's why I've come. You're no longer capable of seeing to the needs of two small, active children. Good Lord, you can't even walk!" her eyes hard as they moved to Murphy. "She can't do 'anything' now, can she?"

"What the hell do you want, Celia? Say it and get out. This is a private party," he growled, "by invitation only."

"Murphy, calm down, please." Beth pleaded. "Celia, we have arranged for help to come in daily. The children will be provided for. Thank you for your concern but as you can see there is no need." Beth's voice was quiet but firm.

"Oh, I see all right. I see plenty. First, you're denying me my rights to visit the children, yet again, while I have to listen to a crippled nobody telling me what I can and cannot do regarding my own flesh and blood!" Celia sneered. "Tell me, Beth, have you ever done anything well or is mediocrity your best feature? I just can't leave my sister's children in such hands!"

"Get out!" Murphy snapped, his face showing his rage.

"Just a minute, love," Beth murmured up at him, "Celia, if you found something about me that was good, say for instance a talent, would you stop causing trouble and sign over the children permanently to Murphy and me?"

"But, of course, but by talent, it can't be making strawberry jam!"

"Of course," Beth agreed, "it would be something else. Would you agree that dancing was a talent? Perhaps if I could play an instrument or sing? Would you accept any of those as a talent worthy of custody, Celia?" her voice deceptively quiet.

"But, of course, but talent as I know it must be recognized by more than your... friends."

"You mean by a nightclub, for instance?" Beth insisted. "If I would sing, for instance, at a recognized club, you would let us have the children?"

"Darling ... " she laughed, "if you were a success at a decent club, I'd gladly sign over the children."

"Johnny, what's the name of the club you're booked at?" Beth asked, her voice shaking slightly.

"The Tower," Johnny said. "If you're sure, Beth, make it the third week in June. I'll play for you." He spoke quietly, knowing what Beth was about to say.

"Beth, you don't need to do this," Murphy spoke quietly beside her.

"Yes, I do, love. Don't you see it solves so many problems? First, we get rid of Celia, but more importantly I can lay my ghosts to rest before we get married." Seeing his concern, she kissed him, gently as much to give him assurance as to gain his strength. "Please, Murphy, with you beside me I can do it. Will you let me try?"

"Oh, Beth," he murmured, kissing her hand, "I love you. Let's lay your ghosts to rest."

"Thank you," she whispered, her eyes luminous. Turning to Celia, she said firmly, "Celia, I'll be singing at The Tower, three weeks from today. Please be there with the papers to give us custody of the children."

"Gladly. I wouldn't miss it for the world dear, but what are you gambling? I lose the kids, what are you going to put up?"

"Celia," Beth spoke quietly. "If I don't succeed, I will have lost my pride, isn't that enough?"

Celia walked to the door; her eyes thoughtful. "If you're a flop dear, I get Marshall's shares in your computer company. Fifty percent of Diamond Enterprises, I believe it's called. Take it or leave it." Her face set in determined lines.

Murphy didn't hesitate, "We'll take it, Celia. Now get out," he said, firmly shutting the door behind her.

"Oh, Murphy, your company!" Beth was distressed. Beth returned his smile, but it didn't quite reach her eyes. Oh, Murphy, she thought, I can't let you down. just can't!

"Let's get this party rolling," Johnny teased and started playing the old favorites. His fingers gliding effortlessly over the keys, his mind was on Beth's challenge.

Later that night, long after their guests had left, Murphy, Beth, Johnny and Uncle Henry sat. "Well, at least now we know Celia wanted the kids for greed, not revenge." Uncle Henry began.

"Is that good or bad?" Johnny quipped.

"Bad," Beth declared, "at least before I sometimes felt she cared for them a little bit. But now ...they're only a means to an end," she shivered. Murphy's arm tightened protectively around her.

"Beth, are you sure this is the way we should go about getting the kids? Don't misunderstand, I have every confidence in your singing, I've even talked to Johnny about getting you over your fears, but I don't know if physically or mentally I want you under the strain of practicing and rehearsing. My God, you've just come out of the hospital. You almost died!" His voice shook with the remembered pain and frustration of those agonizing hours.

"Murphy, I'm fine or I will be as soon as these casts come off in two weeks. Don't go back, think of now, of how we are." Beth's face turned upwards; her lips parted as he kissed her gently.

"Gosh, I'm tired, Uncle Henry!" Johnny grinned. "I think it's time we went to bed. Although I doubt, I'll get much sleep with you snoring!"

"I don't snore!" Henry refuted, rising from his chair.

"Well, of course, you're asleep, how would you know?" Johnny teased. "But just this morning Mike was asking if there were any bears about. He had heard one last night in bed." He winked at Beth as he walked up the stairs with Henry, a gentle banter all the way.

"Thank you, Johnny," Murphy whispered as he folded Beth in his arms, for a much-awaited kiss. His hands moving across her back, slowly, pressing her slim body against his own. The kiss deepened as his hands touched the swell of her breast. He pushed her gently away, his breath harsh, as he smiled at her heavy-lidded eyes. "Something tells me this is going to be an extremely long month," he groaned.

Impishly Beth ran her fingertips over his chest, "I do get my casts off in two weeks," she said demurely.

"Vixen," Murphy laughed. "But I'll bear it in mind." He drew her back into his arms and stood up, cradling her head against his shoulder. "Bedtime, love ... and unfortunately, sleep!"

The next two weeks followed a simple pattern with Maria's help. Beth spent her days reading to Mike and Jenny and watching them play with the Brown children. Dusty would join in, his legs growing faster than his

166

body, making him appear clumsy as he ran and jumped. The kittens were no longer containable in the shed and their mews could be found in the garage, on the porch, and especially Dusty's doghouse.

Beth would sing with Johnny in the morning before he left. Rehearsing their old songs, her voice as soft as an echo. Each day gaining confidence that she could do it. Each day bringing her closer to her debut.

Uncle Henry went back home but promised to return for her opening night and wedding. Murphy spent long hours coping with the farm and his business. Trying to successfully run the company by phone. The day her casts came off, Beth was in high spirits as she walked slowly beside Murphy to the car. They joked as they stopped for lunch, treating Mike and Jenny to their favorite burger and fries.

They walked into the house, quiet except for the insistent ringing of the phone. "I'll get it," Murphy said as he strode ahead. "Hello...yes ...what? Well, did you ask Fairfax? No, it's not your fault. I'll be there as soon as I can."

He put the phone down, his eyes traveling to a quiet Beth, leaning against the door. Her hair falling in soft waves about her shoulders, she smiled, "What's wrong?"

"There was a mix-up at the factory. The wrong discs were used causing a short. I can fix it in a few days, or we hire someone who's unfamiliar with the system and it will take even longer."

"See what happens when you're indispensable?" Beth smiled, but her eyes remained serious. "How long will you be gone?"

"A few days hopefully, no more than four at most." He smiled, "I'll be here for your opening night come hell or high water." He kissed her upturned mouth, lingering. Beth felt the old weakness in her knees, and she clutched at his shirt, clinging to him. He raised his head, "Two thousand miles is probably the only thing that would keep me from sharing your bed, maybe it's a good thing I'm going."

"Don't you believe it," Beth murmured against his ear, "hurry back, love, I'll be waiting."

Murphy groaned. "Now how am I to concentrate on fixing that system if all I can think about is you waiting for me?"

"Use it as an incentive to hurry home," Beth teased.

"You won't overdo while I'm gone?" Murphy grew serious, "Where's Johnny? He can keep an eye on you while I'm gone. I'll feel better at least knowing he's here." He looked deep into her eyes; his forehead creased in thought. "You are so beautiful, so very dear to me. Heaven help me if anything should ever happen to you."

Several hours later, he was on a plane. The house seemed so quiet without him Beth thought as she walked through the rooms. Oh, Murphy, please hurry back. She sat at the piano, idling at the keys, humming to herself, a deep fear already clutching at her heart. "If I should fail, Murphy will lose half his company to Celia. Would he still be able to love me ...marry me if I am the cause of his losing his company to Celia? What if I freeze, she thought, remembering the panic rising in her throat from the past, even at the airport amongst a large crowd of people. Beth looked down at the piano, her hands now motionless. A tiny drop of water fell to the keys and was joined by another and yet another. Slowly she lowered her head to rest on her arms and wept.

Johnny found her there still sobbing. He lowered himself to the bench and gathered her into his arms. "Oh Beth, go ahead and cry." He rocked her in his arms, as he had when she was small. Several minutes later, he wiped her eyes and smiled. "Well, I'm glad that's over with! We, dear sister, have work to do. You've had a good cry, now no more. You will not look back on how you were. We're going forward. You are going to be a huge success because of three things. One," he said, counting his fingers as he talked, "you have a fabulous pianist. That's me, of course!" Beth managed a grin. "Two, your voice is an instrument. You can sing like an angel and you're going to because of reason number three," he paused, "you are not going to let Murphy's company or Mike, or Jenny go to Celia. Come Saturday night you are going to close your eyes and instead of The Tower you'll be singing to Murphy, from your heart to his."

Beth took a deep, steadying breath, "Well, thanks big brother." She leaned over and kissed his cheek.

"Now don't go trying to flirt with me, young lady. We've work to do." He showed mock concern. "We need to select our songs and then you'll need a dress. First, we shop for the dress. Off you go, I'll give you ten minutes, or I'll buy one without you!" Beth headed for the stairs, determination in her walk.

Beth stood in her room looking at the girl in the mirror. She seemed almost a stranger, so cool and calm. Her hair had been pulled back from her face and up off her slender neck emphasizing her high cheekbones and large eyes. Small ringlets of hair fell at her ears. The dress left one shoulder bare, its white simple Grecian lines taking advantage of her rounded curves. Beth looked like a princess, beautiful, poised. The mirror did not reveal her inner turmoil. Murphy had been delayed; it was Saturday night. Beth closed her eyes. Oh, please, let me do this for us ...for Murphy. Please help me. I can't let them down, Murphy most of all."

A knock on the door had her heart leaping, "Murphy?" she asked, holding her breath.

"Sorry, love, it's only me," Johnny said, knowing she was disappointed. "Wow! Is this my little sister? You won't have to sing, just stand up and smile. They'll have to pick them up off the floor."

"Well, it would certainly make things simpler," Beth said. "Johnny, you don't think anything's happened to Murphy, do you? All that electrical equipment, it's dangerous!"

"He's fine. He's one man who knows how to take care of himself. He's also a man of his word. Yesterday when he called, he told you he'd be here. He will be." Johnny assured her. "Now we need to leave, he'll know to meet us at the Tower... ready?"

"As I'll ever be," Beth murmured, and proceeded him down the stairs.

Kissing Jenny and Mike goodnight and trying to act as if everything was perfectly normal was very hard. But neither the children nor Casey noticed her nervousness.

"You're like the angel I saw first time I met you, Miss Beth," Casey said, quite moved by her appearance.

"Thank you," Beth smiled, "wish me luck. We'll see you later." She blew them a kiss and walked silently to the car.

Johnny kept up a light conversation, teasing, making outrageous statements, trying very hard to make her relax. It seemed to Beth the drive to the Tower was over before it began. Hand in hand, they walked in the door and up the elevator.

The Tower was a dinner theater high above St. Louis. The circular building housed many other businesses, only the top floor was The Tower. It was designed to make the entire floor revolve. At night the walls of clear windows showed the lights of St. Louis against a sky filled with twinkling stars. The magnificent Gateway Arch seemed to glimmer, looming over the Mississippi River far below. So slowly did the Tower turn, one had the feeling of floating through space, weightless, motionless as the panorama of the entire city played beneath the building. The inside of the Tower was dimly lit, the ceiling lights mirrored the twinkling of stars, almost as if there was no ceiling. It was breathtaking and for a moment Beth was so enchanted as to forget her debut.

"Oh, Johnny," Beth murmured, "it's so beautiful!"

"A fitting background for tonight's star," he said gallantly. Then cupped her chin in his hand, "Are you nervous?"

"Petrified!" she whispered.

"Just remember, you're not here, you're just singing to Murphy, you and he alone. He'll hear you wherever he is. You'll feel him here with you, sing to him, Beth. Remember ...from your heart to his." He kissed her cheek and squeezed her hands before he walked to the piano against one wall of the room.

"Good evening, ladies and gentlemen," a strange voice began. "Welcome to the Tower. We are very

171

privileged to have as our host this evening, a very talented pianist...Johnny Duncan."

There was a round of applause as Johnny bowed and sat down, playing the piano as if possessed. The entire room was silenced by the music which flowed through his fingers. As song followed song, the audience responded. Johnny had never played so well. How long he played, Beth had no idea, swept up in the tide of emotion the music aroused.

When the music stopped, the applause was deafening as Johnny bowed, his pleasure at their reception evident. He took the microphone in his hands, "Thank you. I have truly enjoyed my time here in your lovely city. To show my appreciation, tonight as my last night, I have a very special gift for you. A few years ago, I had the privilege of working with a young singer. Tonight, she has consented to sing again with me. With great pride and pleasure, I introduce Elizabeth Whitaker."

Beth moved as if in a trance to stand beside Johnny, who was adjusting the microphone for her. He turned and whispered, "for Murphy," and walked to the piano.

As he began playing the introduction to the songs, Beth closed her eyes to shut out the people, the noise and to picture Murphy sitting before her. Her first notes were soft, barely heard above the piano. But as the song progressed, her lovely voice echoed the magical notes of the piano. Her eyes opened. So real did her image of Murphy look that Beth felt as if he were real. Then he smiled, and Beth's voice erupted into an enchantment of sound. Her melodies capturing the hearts of all, she sang as Johnny had told her ... from her heart to his. As the final notes echoed through the air, a silence filled the room only to explode minutes later in a deafening applause. Tears fell unheeded down her cheeks as she bowed her head in recognition of their praise. But the crowd was not to be denied. When she walked slowly to the door, the applause grew louder as shouts of "Encore!" filled the room. Strong arms crushed her to him as she approached the door. "You were fabulous, my darling," he whispered into her hair, feeling the soft trembling body against his own.

"Oh, Murphy," Beth sobbed, "I wanted you to be here so badly. I thought for a moment that perhaps I had dreamed up your image. But then you smiled. I felt I could do anything for you. I've missed you so much."

"No more than I have." He kissed her eyelids and then her lips. "I love you so much, it felt like years that I had seen you, held you in my arms. I only finished this morning. I took the only flight available. There wasn't time to call and let you know I'd be late and would meet you here." Again, he kissed her, crushing her to him. When he lifted his head to look upon her shining eyes, he drew a ragged breath.

Johnny appeared, grinning from ear to ear, "Hey you two, I hate to break it up but if Beth doesn't reappear for an encore, I think they'll tear the place apart. Besides which you might like to catch an angry Celia heading towards the exit."

Johnny took Beth's hand and led her back to the piano. As the audience saw her return, their applause continued. Johnny again took the microphone. "Thank you ... thank you." As they quieted, "I failed to mention in Beth's earlier introduction that I think she's very special, too. This beautiful, talented young lady is my favorite little sister."

Beth grinned, leaned over to add, "Johnny, I'm your ONLY sister!" The audience laughed, aware of the love between these two talented performers. "Our encore is a medley Beth and I wrote many years ago. I hope you enjoy it."

Once more Beth listened to her introduction, but this time she didn't feel nervous, only very happy. Her happiness showed in her eyes as they shone much like the stars outside the window. She sang this time to the people in the room. smiling as her eyes went from one table to the next, a special happiness upon finding the table where a proud Uncle Henry sat beside a beaming Miss Lucy.

Again, the applause was thunderous, as Johnny and Beth bowed and left the stage. Murphy waited, triumphantly waving the legal paper with Celia's signature.

Johnny grinned as he shook Murphy's hand, leaving the car keys as he did. "I think I'll ride home with Henry and Miss Lucy. You don't mind taking Beth home for me?"

"Thanks, Johnny," Murphy smiled.

"Just name your first child after me!" Johnny said as he squeezed Beth's hand. "You were unbelievable. You stole the show. I'm very proud of you, it took a lot of guts to do what you did tonight." He hugged her and then disappeared into the crowd.

Murphy took Beth's hand, "Let's go home."

Beth leaned against his shoulder as he threaded the car through the traffic. "How about something to eat?" Murphy asked.

"I'd love to. I don't think I've had anything to eat all day. Suddenly I'm starved!"

"Does it matter what or where?"

"Only as long as I'm with you. I'll even settle for one of those burgers and fries Mike and Jenny are crazy about!"

"Somehow," Murphy laughed, "I can't envision you in that dress eating French fries!"

"You don't like my dress?" she teased.

"You look sensational and you know it! But then I'm inclined to think you look good wearing anything."

"That love, is because you're prejudiced! Thank heavens! Oh, Murphy, I was so afraid without you there."

"But I came. I told you I'd be there, Beth. Nothing could have kept me away tonight."

"It's all over, the kids are really ours?"

"All signed and officially sealed. Henry saw to that and Miss Lucy witnessed. There's only one problem remaining. Beth, do you want to continue singing? They loved you back there. They'll be asking you to come back and there'll be others. You are so talented. I don't want to take you away from all the success that could be, would be yours."

"Murphy, are you saying you want me to continue singing professionally even after we're remarried?"

"God, Beth! I'd hate the separations. I'd resent your time away from me, our children. I'd be lying if I said I didn't want you at home beside me. But more than that I want you happy. I saw how radiant you were tonight singing. I can't take that away from you."

Beth chuckled," Oh, darling, for being so smart, sometimes you're awfully dense. Of course, I was radiant. You were there. Of course, I was happy. I had laid my ghosts to rest. I felt complete again, no more fears to plague me, but more importantly I was happy because I didn't let you down. If Celia had been able to get the shares of your company, how could I have faced you knowing I had lost some of what you have poured your life into! And there's Jenny and Mike. Murphy, I love them so much, if we were to lose them, I'd feel as if we lost our own children. Is it any wonder I was happy? Radiant?"

"But what about the future, Beth? Can you be content to be just my wife, just a mother? Wouldn't you feel resentful for having to lead such a quiet life?"

"Has it been quiet since we've lived here? Something is always happening! And when we add to our menagerie with other children, I want more than anything else to hold your child in my arms. How could I leave my life for someone else to do? Murphy, my happiness lies in being with you as your wife, as the mother of your children, not in singing. I can sing at home, in church and sometimes maybe even sing with Johnny for special occasions. But when I do, I want you beside me and when we're done, we'll go home together. Don't you see, love, I don't want anything other than to be with you."

Tears filled her eyes, as she struggled to convince Murphy, feeling as if her future happiness depended on it. Murphy was silent, as he drove the rest of the way to Elsah. He drove past the familiar stores and streets, following the winding, narrow road. But instead of turning off into their lane, he continued further into the dark, wooded cliffs and hills beyond. Suddenly, he stopped and without a word, climbed and helped Beth out as well. He led her a few steps and stopped; a panorama displayed before her. Far beneath their feet lay the rivers of the Mississippi and Missouri. From the point where they stood, they saw the merging of their waters, the star-studded sky reflected in their depths. A far-off horn sounded as the lights winked against the darkness. Trees leaned low on the banks, their sweeping branches touching, protecting as the surging rivers flowed past.

Murphy's hands rested on Beth's shoulders, holding her against him, their bodies touching yet apart. "When my mother left my father, it was because being a wife and mother weren't enough." He paused, breathing in the cool moist air from the river, "Later all the women I met let it be known that for them being a wife and mother were not enough." He turned her towards him, looking deep into her eyes. "Is it any wonder that I'd question your future as being only a wife and mother?"

Beth drew a deep breath, her eyes never wavering as they returned Murphy's searching gaze, "If I were only a wife and mother, Murphy, you're right it would not be enough." His indrawn breath showed the pain that crossed his face. "But I won't be just a wife. I'll be your helpmate, your friend, your lover. To our children, I won't be just their mother. I'll be their teacher, their guide, their friend. Not just any wife, Murphy, but yours."

Her voice, little more than a whisper, filled his heart with joy as he understood the sincerity and the truth of her words. He gathered her up in his arms gently, protectively. "Oh Beth, tonight you sang, and I will remember. But your words just now were like a song to my heart. A song I'll remember ever more." His lips claimed hers in a kiss to seal their new closeness and understanding. Together they stood high above the cliffs and watched the timeless rivers fade into the night.

EPILOGUE

Father Mac's voice rose above the distressed cries of the tiny baby held in Johnny's arms. "I baptize you Matthew John Whitaker, in the name of the Father, the Son and the Holy Spirit." As the ceremony drew to a close, relief flooded Johnny's face as he handed the baby back to his grinning parents.

"Well, Johnny, what did you do to him?" Murphy chuckled as tiny Matthew stopped crying in his mother's arms.

"How do you stand it? At least with a radio I can turn it off! I swear all I did was hold him!"

"You held him all right, like a delicate porcelain vase!" Beth retorted. "Babies like to be held securely, snuggled close to your body, don't you love?" she asked the smiling baby.

"I'll tell you what, you take the babies, I'll have my kids when they're six or seven years old like Mike and Jenny. That's the way to have kids." Johnny grinned, hoisting both children in his arms. "When they're this big, I can throw them around just like a sack of potatoes!"

"Am I a lump like 'taters, Uncle Johnny?" a giggling Jenny asked.

"Not yet, but after I drop you a couple of times you will be!" Johnny assured her.

Fresh laughter echoed across the orchards as they walked back to the farm. Beth and Murphy watched as Johnny, Jenny and Mike ran ahead, Dusty barking at their heels. Casey walked more slowly, and followed together with Uncle Henry, no doubt discussing whatever proud uncles talk about at baptisms.

Murphy lifted the sleeping bundle from Beth and very gently peered under the blanket. The round little face with the dark curls, sucked on his thumb oblivious to the joy on his father's face. He turned to Beth, a dark gleam in their depths as he saw the radiance in her face.

"Are you happy?" he asked softly, his lips touching her temple as she straightened the blanket around their son.

"Oh, Murphy, I am so delirious with joy, do you even need to ask?"

"NO, I see it in your eyes, your face as you care for all those around you. This past year has been the happiest of my life. From the first time I saw you coming up the steps of the courthouse, so beautiful, so fresh, my heart has never been the same. As beautiful as you were the first time, when we were remarried at St. Mary's, you were even more radiant, more breathtaking. I can still see you walking up the aisle, the flowers in your hair, you seemed to float into my arms. Waking beside you each morning, holding you in my arms each night, watching our child grow inside you and to hold this tiny infant in my arms, a sign of our love." He breathed deeply, "Beth, I will thank God every day for the rest of my life and beyond that he sent you to me."

Beth's eyes filled with tears, as she stood on tiptoe to kiss her husband, touched by his words, spoken from his heart to hers. His words...a song to her heart from his heart ... a song she would always remember.

The End

Note from the Author

I want to personally thank you for your time and effort in the reading of this book. I love writing, and I owe it to my readers to do the best I can. The best source of input to influence my future efforts is your feedback. Please take just a few minutes to share whatever thoughts you may have on this book by going to https://www.amazon.com/author/m_dipaolo and submit a rating and, if you wish, some comments as well. I would really appreciate it.

ABOUT THE AUTHOR

Marcella (Marky) DiPaolo was raised as a farm girl in Moro, Illinois. She was one of six children, and they all interacted daily with their loving parents and grandparents who served as ideal role models for them as they grew up on the farm. Upon graduating from high school, Marcella started her career in business. She also went to college, initially to become an accountant. It was in the business world that she met the person with whom she wanted to share the rest of her life.

It didn't take long for the young couple to start filling up their home with children. It was in the raising of her own that she realized that working with kids was her passion. She decided that teaching was the direction she wanted to go. During the early years, she was the one that stayed home to watch the kids while her husband worked during the day and went to school at night to complete his education. Once finished, he spent his evenings with the children, so she could go on and complete her BA in Elementary Education and later getting a Masters with a concentration in mathematics.

After more than thirty-five years of teaching, she recently retired but continues to teach from time to time as a substitute at a local parochial school. Over the years, Mrs. D., as she is referred to by her students, was recognized for her teaching accomplishments having received several awards and other forms of recognition. 'Mrs. D' has certainly had a very special effect on a lot of young people, all of whom she still considers members of her 'extended' family.

Marcella has a lot of other interests as well. In addition to a voracious appetite for romantic plots and characters, she is also fond of adventure stories and mysteries. She also loves to watch sports, play golf, eat chocolate, and spend as much time as possible with her family.

Marcella's love of reading began at a very early age. However, she never dreamed she might become a writer until much later in life. Being somewhat addicted to historical romances, both in books and on the screen, she has been exposed to a lot of writing styles. This experience and her time on the farm, raising a family, and all those years in the classroom have provided her with a wealth of ideas to apply to her writing career.

Other Books Written by Marcella DiPaolo

Clear Water Bride Series
    Bargain Bride
    Troubled Bride
    Forgotten Bride
    Reluctant Bride
    Runaway Bride
Morgan Brothers Storm Series
    Above the Storm
    After the Storm
    Beyond the Storm
Pine City Chance Series
    Taking a Chance
    A Second Chance
Other (Not Part of a Series)
    Promises to Keep